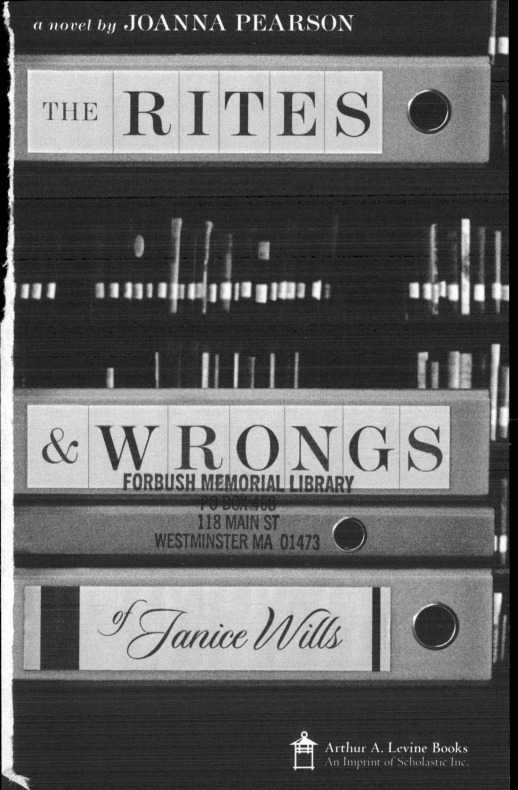

a novel by JOANNA PEARSON

THE RITES

& WRONGS

of Janice Wills

Arthur A. Levine Books
An Imprint of Scholastic Inc.

Pearson, Joanna.
    The rites and wrongs of Janice Wills / Joanna Pearson. — 1st ed.
        p. cm.
    ISBN 978-0-545-19773-1 (hardcover : alk. paper) —
[1. Coming of age — Fiction.   2. Anthropology — Fiction.
3. Interpersonal relations — Fiction.   4. High schools — Fiction.
5. Schools — Fiction.   6. Family life — North Carolina — Fiction.
7. North Carolina — Fiction.]   I. Title.
    PZ7.P323135Rit 2011
    [Fic] — dc22
                                                                    2010029348

10 9 8 7 6 5 4 3 2 1   11 12 13 14 15

Printed in the U. S. A.   23
First edition, July 2011

For my mom, Judy Pearson, who would want me to tell you that she is *truly* nothing like the mother in this book, and for my nana, Jo Whisenant, who has always been ready and willing to dance.

The Anthropological Headquarters of
Janice H. Wills
Melva, North Carolina

Mark Aldenderfer, PhD
Editor
Current Anthropology

Dear Dr. Aldenderfer,

I write to you from my anthropological research
station in Melva, North Carolina, where I have been deeply
engaged studying the cultures, behaviors, and rituals of
the American adolescent in the small-town South — a
strange and fascinating creature, I'm sure you'll agree.
I submit the enclosed field notes in hopes that my
findings may be of interest to you and to the readers of
Current Anthropology. I believe there are several
anthropological breakthroughs contained in these pages.

Yes, it is true that I am only an adolescent myself,
but I ask you: Who better to approach this subject? I am
truly immersed in the cultures that I study, being both
the observer and the observed. Although I do not yet have
my PhD in anthropology, I am a member in good standing of
both Beta Club and National Honor Society here at Melva
High School. I've done extensive research on my own and
am something of an old-fashioned autodidact.

Please see my findings enclosed. I very much look
forward to your feedback.

Sincerely,
Janice H. Wills
Anthropologist

ANTHROPOLOGICAL
OBSERVATION #1:

*Adolescence provides the female with ample opportunity to appear ugly
and awkward as part of numerous socially mandated rituals. These rituals are perpetuated by adult women, who consider such events to be part
of their "community heritage." In other words, the insult was once inflicted
upon them, and so must in turn be inflicted upon their own daughters.*

Like most girls in my hometown, I had to face the Miss
Livermush Pageant when I was around seventeen years old. Sixteen years and ten months, to be exact. Thus for purposes of
anthropological comparison:

I. Were my name Janice Garcia Lopez instead of
   Janice Wills, already I might have been ushered
   into womanhood through a quinceañera cele-
   bration on my fifteenth birthday. In a flounced
   white dress, my hair in perfect ringlets, I'd have
   performed a choreographed dance with my court
   of attendants and smiled for a gazillion photos
   snapped by my adoring aunts and female cousins.

2. Were I Jewish, around age thirteen, I might have
   had a bat mitzvah, at which I would have read

Hebrew aloud before dancing my feet off at the party held afterward, preferably with Justin Timberlake as the featured entertainment.

3. Were I the son of a noble Japanese samurai family during the Heian era, this year I would have received my adult clothing and hairstyle during the *genpuku* (or *kakan*) ceremony at the shrine of my patron *kami*.

4. Were I a daughter of a Bambuti hunter-gatherer in the Congo, I would already have been married for several years by now, as arranged through a sister-exchange (i.e. my husband would have had to offer his sister or other female relative to a male in my family for marriage too. Like trading teenaged livestock).

Instead, I was an early-twenty-first-century middle-class Protestant girl of Western European descent living in a small town in the southern region of the United States of America. Nearing the end of my junior year at Melva High School, I had two coming-of-age rituals to look forward to:

I. The aforementioned Melva's Miss Livermush Pageant and corresponding Livermush Festival, where the community celebrates everyone's favorite pork liver–based processed meat by marching twenty young women in ridiculous dresses across a stage, and

2. the accompanying Livermush Festival Dance, which holds the place of sociocultural importance that the prom might hold for adolescents in certain other cultures.

I would also add a possible third thing to the list — a secret goal that could make my entire high school experience worthwhile:

3. Publishing an article in *Current Anthropology* before I graduated from high school, thus becoming the youngest person to have done so and legitimizing myself as a scholar in the field.

Because what was my thing — my talent, my one true joy — you ask, having already gathered that being marched across a stage in a ridiculous dress was clearly *not* it? Observing people, that's what. Anthropology, that's what. Anthropology — what our friend Merriam-Webster describes as "the science of human beings; *especially*: the study of human beings and their ancestors through time and space and in relation to physical character, environmental and social relations, and culture." If you want the all-time best self-taught anthropologist under the age of eighteen, I'm your girl.

• • •

My real coming-of-age began on a bright April Saturday in Melva, North Carolina. The morning air was sweet with hydrangea blossoms, and the carefully manicured gardens of our neighbors were studded with red, heavy-headed tulips. Nosy Mrs. Crandor across the street was outside in little plastic gardening clogs, already at work in her flower beds. The other houses — neat, modest multibedroom homes with basketball hoops and clean cars in the driveways — remained quiet. My best friend, Margo, had slept over, and now we sat on the porch swing, staring speechless at the hypnotic sight in front of us.

A flubbery, middle-aged woman was dancing, right there on our front porch. She had platinum-dyed hair and teeth white enough to blind small children. She did a little skip to the left, hopped two-three, and then skipped to the right, her hands held forward like paws, her gold bracelets jangling. The old boards of the porch creaked as she bounded from foot to foot. The woman looked like a lunatic. The woman was my mother.

"It's called the Pony, girls!" my mom panted, skipping from side to side. "I loved this dance! My friends and I did it to so many songs back at my Miss Livermush dance, they had to stop the music and force us to do the grand march!"

Margo collapsed onto me, hooting with laughter. "It's awesome, Mrs. Wills! Keep dancing!" she managed to gulp. Mrs. Crandor looked up from her garden and squinted at us.

"Oh, I could still do it all night, girls! All night! I've still got it in me!" She tilted her head back, a bead of sweat zipping down her forehead, her eyes gleaming with lunacy. "Whoo! Yeah!" my mom shouted to herself. "Keep on! Keep on doing the Pony, Sandra!"

I smacked my hand on my forehead so hard my hand stung. "My God, Mom! Jeez, you have GOT to stop!"

ANTHROPOLOGIST'S NOTE:
My mom is obsessed with this dance, the Pony. Any dance historians among you will note that the Pony

The Pony

In a one-two-three, one-two-three rhythm:

1. Jump lightly off the left foot,
2. to the right forefoot,
3. and back to the left foot,
4. to the full right foot,
5. then the left forefoot,
6. and finish on the right foot.

peaked in popularity nationwide in 1962, well before my mom's own adolescence. It remains unclear whether my mom's belated Pony obsession stems from the fact that a) trends only ever make their way to Melva decades too late or b) my mom herself is stubbornly old-fashioned and *would* be the type of person who was doing a dance from the early '60s that her own mom taught her while everyone else was practicing his moonwalk.

ADDITIONAL NOTE:

The 1960s Pony dance = a wholesomely old-fashioned dance, not to be confused or associated with the 1996 R&B single "Pony" by Ginuwine. It's a different thing altogether, trust me. My mom once made that mistake and found the experience "much more scandalous."

Margo, still giggling, tugged my shirt. "Relax, Jan. Your mom is awesome — she's got spunk!"

I groaned. Mom frowned mid-Pony, right arm up, left arm down. A strand of platinum hair concealed one heavily masca-raed eye. "Janice, you've got to stop that. All that God- and Jesus-ing." She brushed the hair away as she spoke, short of breath. "I'm sure Jesus has better things to worry about, but people in Melva don't. They'll say you're impolite."

"The only thing impolite is the truth: You can't dance!"

Margo laughed and jumped up from the swing, shaking her

dark head of curls. She was wearing one of her signature ensembles: paint-spattered overalls and a floral shirt — what I referred to as her Suburban-Graffiti-Artist-Just-Woken-from-Nap look. "Come on, I'm starving. We need to go inside and make pancakes now before my stomach consumes itself."

It was a Pancake Saturday, a tradition that Margo and I had created when neither of us were invited to Rachel Tedder's spend-the-night party in seventh grade. Rachel and her family had long since moved to Alabama, but we always toasted her with our orange juice glasses on Pancake Saturdays. She'd been the unwitting force that had cemented Margo's and my friendship, after all.

I had met Margo the first day of middle school. There, in the lonely, teeming cafeteria, she had smiled and cleared a space for my tray on the lunch table when I, a shipwrecked sailor on the social seas, asked quietly if I could pull up a chair. I'd liked Margo from the beginning because of her face — it was an open face with a mouth that always seemed to be on the brink of laughter. Meanwhile, the other girl sitting at the lunch table, Rachel Tedder, had arranged her impeccably prepared feta salad with low-cal dressing and diet soda — she was always wise beyond her years when it came to obsessions — while predicting two things:

1. that she, Margo, and I would be best friends from then on, and

2. that when we grew up, Margo would become a famous actress, Rachel would be a successful doctor/fashion designer/businesswoman, and I would enjoy a fulfilling career as an editor of science textbooks.

Rachel had been right — about Margo and me being best friends, at least. Rachel herself ditched us by the time we hit seventh grade, floating effortlessly upward through the higher social strata of baton girls and dance squad girls after deciding we weren't worth her time. One fateful Friday, Margo and I, waiting for our rides by the side of the middle school gym, saw a group of girls all climb giggling into Rachel's mom's van with overnight bags. I'd watched them in silent disbelief — Rachel had always invited *us* to her spend-the-nights! — until I noticed that tears were brimming in Margo's eyes. "You can come to my house," I'd said to Margo, before adding for some reason, "and we'll have a BETTER spend-the-night party, with pancakes for breakfast in the morning and everything." Margo and I had been best friends ever since, just as had been originally foretold. (Unfortunately, Rachel's partial predictive powers now left me worrying about a lonely destiny of mitochondria and cell cycles. An editor of science textbooks?!)

Other than our mutual seventh-grade rejection, I wasn't sure why Margo and I got along so well. Maybe because Margo didn't seem to register whether something was cool or dorky, she was less aware of all those tricky social categories in which people get stuck. I liked this about her. I liked how she simply found things interesting or didn't — and I liked that she found *me* interesting. We hung out a lot, but we also still gathered at least one Friday a month to watch movies, spend the night, and make elaborate pancake breakfasts the next morning. It would be embarrassing if the Hipster Hippies or Future Fashionistas at school ever found out about it, so we referred to it simply as "PS."

ANTHROPOLOGIST'S NOTE:
Pancakes in various forms have been enjoyed across many cultures and featured in cookbooks from as early as 1430. We were engaging with a diverse culinary tradition.

We walked inside to get the pancakes started. My mom followed us into the kitchen. "Janice never has a boyfriend, and now I really see why," she called from behind the refrigerator door. "A sour attitude."

"Thanks, Mom. I call it honesty."

"Or maybe that sour attitude is only directed at me. I wonder. So, which lucky boys are y'all considering as your Miss Livermush escorts? You know you can confide in me. I just want us all to have some girl talk! Over pancakes!"

My dad, carrying the newspaper, poked his head into the kitchen. Seeing us, he nodded quickly before darting back to the living room — my dad tended to avoid Pancake Saturdays due to a) his shyness and b) the excessive amount of estrogen. He retreated to the living room, where I could hear my two little brothers cackling over Saturday morning cartoons.

"We'll be fine without your help on the pancakes, Mom."

"What about Stephen Shepherd, Janice? He's such a doll-baby! Such a cute boy, and with good manners!"

FACT:

Stephen Shepherd had a scattering of long, curling whiskers sprouting randomly all over his chin, and teeth that were always caked with orange crud from cheese puffs. He played Dungeons & Dragons neither ironically nor secretively, and had once (recently) worn a cape to school. This was the type of guy my mom figured I'd like, and this worried me.

The guys — okay, the *guy* — I actually liked was brooding, aloof, and handsome, and he didn't know my name. Or of my existence. This also worried me.

"Mom, I've already told you: I don't need an escort because I do *not* plan to participate in Miss Livermush. Really! Please stop bringing it up!" I said.

Margo poured pancake flour, added an egg and some milk, and began to stir. "Well, it could be fun. We've been watching the pageant since we were little girls," she said, stirring the pancake batter rhythmically, "and since we're juniors, this is our *only* chance at Miss Livermush. It's kind of a milestone. Like being a princess or something for one evening. Or like going back in time — being Scarlett O'Hara."

"Scarlett O'Hara ended up miserable, remember?"

Margo *hmmph*ed and kept stirring.

"She was Machiavellian. Cutthroat. And she wore curtains," I added.

"Lots of romance and great parties," Margo countered.

"Lots of misfortune."

"Janice, you won't end up miserable, and you won't have to wear curtains either," Margo said. "It'll be fun if we do it together! And we don't need dates or escorts or whatever for the dance. We can just go with each other."

"You could win the pageant, you know," I said to Margo. And she could. She was beautiful and talented and, best of all, did not actually care about things like winning Miss Livermush — which somehow made her seem all the more deserving. "I'll root for you. I'll cheer really loud on the sidelines and take notes whenever the other girls mess up. Then, just in case the judges make a mistake, I'll have proof you were the best."

"Oh, honey," my mom interjected, "taking part in Miss Livermush is so special! It's a memory you'll treasure for the rest of your life! I still remember, for *my* Melva's Miss Livermush Pageant, I had on my mother's pearl necklace and little drop pearl earrings, my white gloves that kept falling a little from the elbows, and oh — my dress! It was —"

"Mom, please! If I'm not cheering on Margo to victory *from the audience*, I'm going to stay home with a bag of M&M's and my books about Australian aborigines. Being in the pageant is a memory I'm happy to skip."

"For a smart person, you say very dumb stuff, Janice," Margo said. "And besides, I thought you'd moved on to the tribes of East Africa now?" She whapped me with a spatula while my mom poured the first pancake onto the sizzling pan.

"True. Peoples of the Horn of Africa, actually. When Mursi girls are fifteen or sixteen years old, their lips are cut and they put in those lip plates — you've seen them in photos, probably — and they can stretch their lip out to fit bigger and bigger plates. That's the socially accepted expression of their adulthood," I said.

Mom shook her head. "Janice, you know people here will wonder if you aren't in the pageant. It's expected. Participating in Miss Livermush is part of being a member of this community. It's part of growing up!"

"Can't I just get a lip plate instead?"

My mom grimaced.

ANTHROPOLOGIST'S NOTE:
Let it be said that to be a sixteen- or seventeen-year-old girl in Melva and NOT participate in the Miss Livermush Pageant is social suicide — at least according to my mom's view of things. According to her, if you don't participate, people will assume that you are either physically incapacitated in some horrendous way, or else a sociopath.

Although I was neither incapacitated nor a sociopath, I did know myself to be the most awkward person in the universe — and this was a fact about which I was certain. My father told me I was his princess. My mother told me I had "pluck." Margo told me I was "funny" and had "pretty eyes" — seeming compliments that I've always recognized as gentle, lethal code words for "hopelessly plain." And I once heard the lady in the juniors' department refer to me as "gangly." My mom later insisted that all supermodels are gangly, and that the lady probably meant it as a compliment. I knew, however, that the lady merely meant I resembled an overgrown praying mantis.

"But you live here," Margo said. "Not the Horn of Africa. And it's not such a big deal just to take part, right?"

I sighed. "I'm telling you both right now," I said, one hand over my heart as if saying the pledge of allegiance, "I hereby declare my refusal to participate in Miss Livermush. It's my personal vision of hell, and you can't make me do it, Mom. Since I will not be participating, I volunteer instead to assist Margo in her efforts to win the competition, thereby upsetting the evil Theresa Rose Venable. Margo, I will officially serve as your handmaiden and spy."

Mom clucked softly to herself and stepped behind me, leaving a pancake to burn while she ruffled my hair.

"Oh, my clever anthropology girl. She can see everything so clearly and yet she can't ever see her own —"

"Ugh, stop it, Mom! Please!" I hissed, elbowing her away. She threw up her hands in exaggerated dismay and returned to the stove.

Margo handed me the napkins. "I guess I won't say no to having a handmaiden," she said. "Nor would I say no to scholarship money. Nor to wiping the smug grin off TR's face."

I took a straight shot of pancake syrup like whiskey and smacked my lips, then offered a shot to Margo, who slung hers back with relish. We smiled, syrup-mouthed, at each other and high-fived.

And I thought then, perhaps foolishly, that that was the last time I'd have to worry about vying to be Miss Livermush.

ANTHROPOLOGICAL
OBSERVATION #2:

In the high school ecosystem, hot, disgruntled theatre guys do not ordinarily engage in direct social transactions with stick-insect nerd-girl anthropologists with excellent mathletic records. Such direct interface between castes is highly unusual and thus worthy of further consideration.

The next day, while waiting for Margo to show up for lunch period, I escaped outside to avoid the mayhem of the cafeteria. It was like bloodthirsty imperial Rome in there, one of my favorite societies to study, but not necessarily to eat lunch with. There were also signs all over the cafeteria now that said "Get Ready for the Annual Livermush Festival!" which weren't exactly appetizing. Besides, it was beautiful outside — the familiar Melva High School buildings set against a blue, cloudless sky.

FACT:
Melva High School is home of the proud Fighting Hummingbirds. State 2A champions in football, tennis, and swimming, depending on the year. Proud constituent of the North Carolina public school system. Big, ugly hunk-a-brick buildings right there at the highway intersection, walking distance to McDonald's, the Tan-A-Lot Spa, Dell's Autowash, and Unyuns Diner.

The opening to the MHS alma mater actually goes "Buzz, buzz, buzz, Melva Hummingbirds! / We loudly sing your praise! / Buzz, buzz, buzz, Melva Hummingbirds! / Look quick! We'll fly away!"

My only claims to fame at Melva High School were having finished fourth for sophomore class president (there had only been four candidates); being captain of the academic quiz team, Hi-Q; and serving as president of Science Club (a group that was, at its most glorious, five members strong). I had once also tried founding the Anthropology Enthusiasts Club, but no one had showed up except for Bobby Whitmore — and everyone knew that Bobby referred to all girls as "ho-bags" and showed up for any after-school activity that he could mock while gobbling all the free snacks.

I opened up my notebook and reviewed the notes I'd compiled that day.

ANTHROPOLOGIST'S NOTES:
MELVA HIGH SCHOOL, A BRIEF TAXONOMY

I. The Smart Pretty (aka Future Businesswoman of America): Adjectives frequently used to describe her include a) prompt b) cheerful c) hardworking d) anal-retentive. She eats Grape-Nuts with soy milk for breakfast every morning at 7:16 while listening to National Public Radio's *Morning Edition*.

She does squats while brushing her teeth and listens to Japanese language lessons on the treadmill. Existing in the middle level of the social ecosystem, the Smart Pretty is hungry for social advancement. Not mean, but often ruthless. Example: Missy Wheeler.

2. The Dumb Pretty: Much like one of the Smart Pretties, only, as the name suggests, dumber. Greater emphasis on makeup. Sense of self-worth more tied to how recently she has shaved her legs. Thinks *Cosmo* is a magazine full of good and reasonable advice. Lower level of the social ecosystem than the Smart Pretty, more harmless, unless adopted into superior clique. Example: Casey Williams (former Dumb Pretty, achieved social ascendancy, and now = Beautiful Rich Girl).

3. The Softball Husky: Enormous calf muscles, maximus gluteus maximus. Thick ponytails. Healthy American farm-girl look with big, tanned shoulders, like she could help you wrestle down your runaway hog in a pinch. She slaps her friends on the back in the hallways. Not typically predatory or powerful in the high school ecosystem, but known to yell at the pathetically nonathletic if, say,

you're on the same volleyball team in PE. Example: Tori Nathans.

4. Hipster Hippie: Artfully scraggle-haired. Often rich. Purchases expensive clothes meant to resemble clothes obtained from a dumpster. Cultivates air of artsiness without ever having made actual art. The rival tribe of the Beautiful Rich Girls — different aesthetic, but similar roles as social power brokers. Example: Darby Hunt, or Madelyn Flynn.

5. Formerly Homeschooled: Denim prairie skirts and year-round candy cane–patterned turtlenecks. Eighties bangs and scrunchies for the girls, center parts for the guys. He or she presents an otherworldly innocence about basic facets of adolescent life and sometimes has difficulty reading the sarcasm in scathing remarks made by members of other groups. Often very good at one particular thing — trombone, chess, physics — and it is this particular interest that has pulled them away from the homeschool cloister. Example: Stephen Shepherd.

6. Beautiful Rich Girl, or BRG: Take TR as an example

The rest of the pages were missing. I shuffled through my notebook before emptying my entire backpack. Where were the rest of my notes? I could hear the blood rushing in my ears like approaching white water. I'd had all my notes last in French class. Tanesha Jones, my favorite French class friend, and I had started to work on our French language skit together. She'd seen one of the pages and said, "Wow! What have you got in there? Secrets of every single social division in Melva High School or what?" I'd made a joke and quickly put the rest of my anthropological notes away. Tanesha and I had worked on our project, I'd gone to other classes, and sometime between then and now, half the notes had disappeared! This couldn't be happening. Suppose Darby Hunt found them? Or worse still — TR? If she found my anthropology notes, I wouldn't survive to see the end of junior year.

I pulled out my Swiss cheese sandwich, hoping I might think clearly once I ate. Or if disaster was imminent, I might as well eat one last meal. I'd just taken a bite when Paul Hansen approached.

"Hey, Janice," he called before plopping down beside me on the grass. He tossed his backpack and a thick book, *A History of God*, down beside him. I raised an eyebrow at the book.

"What? It's interesting," Paul said, nodding at it. "Besides, I already read up on the history of the devil. So many depictions of the devil over the years — you've got your witch trials, you've got your *Paradise Lost*, you've got your *Rosemary's Baby* — it's fascinating."

I exhaled loudly — for Paul's benefit. "And yet you still haven't realized how fascinating anthropology is," I said.

He smiled, pulling out his lunch from a bag. "I'm leaving that to you. This town's only got room for one anthropologist."

We sat there for a minute in silence, each chewing our food thoughtfully. Paul was my good friend, but he was prone to passing obsessions. Recently there had been the political activist spell, during which he tried to drop out of school to campaign for the Democratic candidate for president; the playwriting interval, when he missed a month of school to finish his masterpiece; the time when he shaved his head to become a Tibetan monk but didn't have money to get to Tibet; his temporary craze for the metaphysical poets. . . . It helped that Paul was a quasi-genius, so he was constantly reading about some new topic — he could become interested in anything — and during each phase, he usually knew what he was talking about. But this faddishness seemed to undermine the legitimacy of his passions, and it annoyed me sometimes, as it suggested that no one our age could actually be serious about something the way I was serious about anthropology. I'd once asked Paul why he always got super-enthusiastic about new things but didn't necessarily keep up with all of them. He'd looked at me with this sad expression and said, "Well, I'm looking for something I can feel, I dunno, passionate about — you know, believe in. Plus, the world is too interesting. I can't help it."

Paul, currently in a raw foods phase, crunched his carrots and sunflower seeds. We were always able to do this with each other, I thought — just sit in silence. Paul and I used to get together to listen to obscure hip-hop or old gospel recordings that he found at yard sales, or whatever it was that he happened to be obsessed with at the time. We'd started a mix CD exchange too, or competition, really. Each of us made mix CDs for the other, striving to outdo the other's best efforts with the most interesting or obscure finds. I liked the comfortable feeling between us, even if we weren't really doing anything.

We hadn't hung out as much this year, though, because Paul now spent all his time with The Girlfriend. The Girlfriend went to the county high school. Her actual name was Susannah. She was delicate and preternaturally pretty, like a girl who should live in a Victorian locket. She added to this effect by wearing high lace collars, vintage patent leather boots, and velvet hair bows. The Girlfriend made these clothes look very artsy and cool, whereas I (and almost anyone else) would have simply looked like my imaginary British great-granny had dressed me for a High Anglican church service.

I thought The Girlfriend was neither mean nor nice — I'd never really heard her talk. I hadn't exactly avoided her, but I hadn't sent the good ship *Friendship* sailing her direction either.

I refocused on the gazebo. I'd seen a particular dark head exit the side door of the school, moving toward it.

ANTHROPOLOGIST'S NOTE:
In many societies, there is a sacred place of reflection reserved for certain members — think sweat lodge or secret society. For MHS, it was the gazebo. The theatre guys stand on the seats with their heads hidden in order

to smoke without being seen. Occasionally a teacher busts them, and no one smokes for a while. Still, they prefer to stand there like that, half-hidden, instead of sitting. And eventually, the smoking starts up again. To outsiders, they appear as a circle of dark-jeaned legs, a low grumble of voices, and the faint whiff of smoke wafting from the cupola.

"I see you looking at him," Paul said. He tossed a carrot. It hit me on the nose.

"Who?"

"Jimmy. That's who."

"Oh, Jimmy Denton? I barely even know him."

"Who are you looking at, then? It's definitely one of the theatre guys in the gazebo."

"Hey, just because those guys are more artistic than anybody else at Melva . . . Besides, I'm not staring at anybody. I was just staring into nowhere. The abyss. The void."

FACT:

I was indeed staring at Jimmy Denton. I'd spent the greater part of sophomore and junior years staring, or longing to stare, at Jimmy Denton. Ever since I'd seen him skipping class to read *Hamlet*, I'd been in love. At the time, the beginning of my sophomore year, I'd been waiting for my mom to pick me up early for a dentist appointment,

and there'd been Jimmy, half-hidden under a tree outside, reading the very play that half the kids in my
English class had refused to finish or had groaned over.
I'd loved *Hamlet*. In fact, I'd been a little bit *in* love with
Hamlet, and so that day, watching Jimmy read, I'd begun
to imagine Jimmy as Hamlet, or vice versa. . . . By the time
he'd nodded at me, I'd already dedicated my first anthropology book to him and named our three future children.
It was insta-love. And it also didn't hurt that Jimmy was
the best actor MHS had ever seen. And the handsomest.

Paul frowned, shook his head, and scooped up the rest of his
food. "Listen, I gotta run inside. I told Stephen I'd return this
DVD of his I borrowed. . . ."

"Stephen Shepherd? The caped crusader of dragons? Mr.
Cheese Puffs Breath?" I asked.

Paul laughed, but not really — it was more just an exhalation
of air. "Yeah, Janice. Stephen Shepherd. He's a nice guy. Smart.
You should actually talk to him sometime."

I looked at him, unsure how to respond. But he jumped onto
his lean runner's legs and was off across the lawn to the cafeteria,
leaving me with half a sandwich and half a view of my crush's
pant legs. *Redirect*, I thought. *Stop looking over at Jimmy in the gazebo.*
There were other, more pressing concerns — like tribal cultures
dying out in Papua New Guinea, my unwritten *Current Anthropology*
article, or, worse yet, my missing anthropology notes on all the

other students at Melva High, notes that were floating danger-ously somewhere around the school. . . .

And that's when Jimmy Denton approached me.

I gazed at him walking toward me the way someone dying of thirst in the desert gazes at a glimmering oasis mirage. Me? Why was Jimmy walking toward me? I squinted to see if it was another one of the theatre guys instead. His face, however, was unmistakable — all brooding and dark-eyed and handsomely sullen. It was not another guy from the gazebo, not a mirage, not a hologram — it was absolutely Jimmy Denton in all his Jimmy Denton-ness.

Jimmy wiped his hands on his T-shirt. It was somehow ter-rifically manly, that gesture, and I wondered why all males are not constantly wiping their hands on their T-shirts. Beneath that T-shirt, he had actual biceps, actual chest muscles — the kind one gets from doing push-ups or, I don't know, lifting bushels of hay and hammering heavy wooden planks. He was still walking toward me. He was *stopping beside me.*

"Hey," he said to me. "You're Janice, right?"

I nodded, swallowing a huge knot of saliva wedged in my throat.

"You and Margo Werther hang out all the time, right? You're the one who's the anthropologist?"

I nodded again, thinking this might be the greatest day of my life so far. Not only did he know my name, he knew that I was an anthropologist?! I felt a little light-headed.

"I found this," he said, pulling a folded wedge of papers from his back pocket. "I'm guessing it's yours."

My hand was clammy as oyster meat as I took the papers from him and opened it up. This is what I read:

of the quintessential Beautiful Rich Girl, or BRG. Certainly this is the ruling caste of Melva High School — BRGs are the taste determiners, the ones with the power to excommunicate someone socially. . . .

The rest of my notes! I flipped through the pages, making sure everything was there. My hand was shaking. Of course Jimmy had known these were mine — I'd idly scrawled my name and initials all over the sheet. "Janice Wills" in bubble letters, "Janice Wills" in all caps, and (oh, God!) "Janice Wills, Anthropologist." *Oh*, I thought. *Oh, no.* If Jimmy didn't hate me, he at the very least must have thought I was a complete dork.

I looked up at Jimmy. "Thanks," I said weakly.

He smiled a half smile at me and shook his head. "No, thank *you*," he said. "It was great reading. Especially the part where you speculate on the inverse relationship between baseball ability and intelligence. Oh, and the part where you argue that certain borderline personality traits are actually just culturally reinforced in theatre kids."

I stared at him.

"Seriously?" I asked. "You're not offended, right? This stuff is, ugh, well, it's just notes. And it's not exactly flattering. I'm a moron to have left it lying around. Oh — you didn't show this to anyone else, did you?"

He laughed. His laugh enveloped me. He smelled faintly of cigarettes and spearmint, and he looked so handsome standing there, his hair tipped by sun, like some beautiful Greek god dropped down in Melva.

"No, relax. It's probably true it's best not to let this fall into just anyone's hands," he said. "But I'm glad I found it. I liked it. Somebody finally speaks truth to Melva High School. You're good. As an anthropologist, I mean."

I stared at him again, unable to thank him for the compliment. Then the moment broke. He wiped his hands again on his shirt.

"Well, anyways. See you around, Janice."

"Thanks again," I said.

"And you and I," he added, turning to go, "we should hang out sometime. We've got more in common than I realized. Compared to everybody else in this place."

"Definitely," I said. "Definitely," I repeated, but he had, like a mirage, already disappeared.

I continued to stare into the absence where Jimmy Denton had just stood. I'd just had an actual conversation with him! And he had actually suggested that we hang out! I wished that Margo had been there to witness this and reassure me it had really taken place.

I whipped my hair over my shoulder the way a beautiful girl would in a shampoo ad. Things felt different. Either I was hallucinating, or it seemed Jimmy Denton liked me, at least a little.

ANTHROPOLOGICAL
OBSERVATION #3:

In smaller adolescent ecosystems, the topic of conversation is invariably that of the adolescent ecosystem itself. Thus, the fewer actual events that occur, the more likely the adolescents in question will talk about one another — a form of modern conversational cannibalism.

By the time I walked outside to find Margo after school, the crowd in the student parking lot was just beginning to thin out. Margo was sitting outside the back entrance, soaking up the late-day heat. A few clusters of lingering students were still hanging out around their cars, flirting or wasting time before sports practice. I threaded my way through a crowd of Goths slouching against cars in guyliner and black pants, Cowboys sporting the fuzzy my-first-mustache look, Dumb Pretties laughing too loudly and wearing scandalously short flounced skirts, Smart Pretties with organized notebooks, quiet voices, and knee-length skirts, Hip-Hoppers encircling one bank of lockers in the corner, a little knot of the Formerly Homeschooled wearing long prairie skirts and off-brand sneakers, and a crew of Football Players crowing loudly at some joke.

"Hey," I called.

Margo looked up at me, smiling. As I approached, I couldn't help questioning my best friend's fashion decisions. Margo's

T-shirt said "Get Funky!" in sparkly letters. It was the sort of shirt a bratty twelve-year-old would beg her mom to buy her from Wal-Mart. Margo was, in my opinion, the prettiest girl at MHS, but she barely ever fixed her hair and tended to dress "thematically" rather than fashionably. Today was one of her ironic looks: a sort of tongue-in-cheek take on the Early '90s Britney Spears–Idolizing Prepubescent Fangirl.

FACT:

Margo is from one of the oldest and most well-established families in Melva, the Werthers. Her ancestors made their fortune in textiles and then rose to a position of enormous political influence throughout both the state and the entire South — although more recently, things had changed for the Werthers. They still had the prestige of their name, but that was about it. They were Melva's threadbare aristocracy — not poor exactly, but definitely not rich. Money aside, Margo has always worn awful clothes on purpose because she just doesn't care. Or, rather, she cares a lot about demonstrating that she does not care.

ANTHROPOLOGIST'S NOTE:

In the art of primitive cultures, breasts and hips were interpreted as signs of fertility. Example: the Woman of Willendorf, a figurine made 24,000 years ago. Margo had the hips, the lips, the butt, and the breasts to be a true fertility goddess, but at Melva High School, these things were interpreted merely as Bad Girl Potential. Either Margo was unaware of this supposed aura of Bad Girl Potential around her, or, as she did with most dumb assumptions, she chose to ignore it.

"Where were you all lunch period?" I asked. "The craziest thing happened! You won't believe who I ended up talking to."

"Oh, crap. Sorry. Chorus. I met Jen to practice for a minute and then we ended up going through lunch. Sorry about that," Margo said, stretching her legs out lazily from the curbside where she sat and fishing around in her purse for a cigarette. She claimed that she tended to smoke only when she was anxious, but I'd noticed that it was mainly just when she was bored. "Who'd you talk to?"

I looked around to see if other people were in listening distance. They weren't, but I still felt nervous speaking Jimmy's name, as if uttering it would conjure him to appear suddenly behind me. "I'll tell you later," I said. "When we're not at school."

"Okay. Still wanna go to the Cellar?" Margo asked.

I nodded. The Cellar was the Mocha Cellar, the only hangout that existed in Melva.

ANTHROPOLOGIST'S NOTE:
As I detail in my most recent essay, "Margaret Mead, Melva, and Me: An Anthropologist Comes of Age in the

Land of Livermush" (currently seeking publication), a town like Melva will often have one establishment that attempts to add a touch of cool, a touch of urbanity. And by this, I mean a pseudo-Starbucks (since Melva doesn't have the economic base to support the prepackaged "cool" of an actual Starbucks) — a weak, watery version of the chain. Teenagers will take over this establishment as their own hangout, driving the adult customers away, and spend long hours but very little money. Said establishment will thus last only one to four years before becoming financially insolvent.

The Mocha Cellar was currently that establishment, and by my watch, it'd be extinct within the next year. As it existed now, it was a dim, grungy basement beneath a sandwich shop that hosted local bands and apparently sold coffee. I'd never actually seen someone drinking coffee there, but everyone in high school went there all the same — to loiter long hours and occasionally gulp down cookies as big as your face and giant, bewhipped milk-shake-type beverages, and of course to escape our parents.

When we got to the Mocha Cellar, I could hear the little cluster of Beautiful Rich Girls, or BRGs, whispering and giggling as soon as we walked in the door. Theresa Rose, Tabitha, and Casey wore ridiculously oversized young-Hollywood sunglasses perched on their heads like headbands. They were all three beautiful in their varied hues — TR was the blonde, Tabitha the dark, high-cheekboned one, Casey the classically pretty brunette.

Being near these girls was like basking in a golden light. Old people looked on and smiled. Happily married Baptist preachers stuttered uncomfortably. Even wobbling toddlers became smitten and clung to them. That was the kind of black magic TR and her crew wielded.

ANTHROPOLOGIST'S NOTE:
Yes, these girls were of a classic type, or stereotype: the beautiful girl bullies, the clique of popular girls, the mean girls. It was like they'd walked right out of a movie — living, breathing caricatures. At least as far as I could tell. In their presence, I felt all my worst physical flaws sharpening into stark focus: My shoulder blades stuck out like a stegosaurus's spines; I had eyebrows like two woolly caterpillars trying to mate; skinny arms; hair the color of paper grocery bags; and the long legs and feet of a frog. . . .

I'd been bursting to tell Margo about my encounter with Jimmy, but now I wanted to wait until the BRGs weren't so close. I'd permanently move to a remote Polynesian village if they ever heard me gushing about Jimmy.

"Who'd you talk to? What was it you were so excited to tell me?" Margo asked.

"Oh, you know," I said quickly, thinking of Jimmy's face and voice while trying to avoid the gaze of the BRGs. "Just things. Always things."

We got glasses of sweet iced tea and took our usual table, but even as we were pulling out our chairs, I felt something — the cold realization that the popular girls' gaze had shifted to us. We'd somehow managed to attract their idling, carnivorous attention.

Theresa Rose called out to us. "Hey, Margo," she said in her syrupy voice, "love the shirt! Very edgy, very fashion-forward!"

ANTHROPOLOGIST'S NOTE:
The leader of the rival tribe offers a challenge. In this setting, that challenge comes in the form of sarcasm: direct address with a wicked mock-compliment.

The BRGs looked at us expectantly, waiting for Margo to respond to TR's comment. Instead, Margo glared at the wall, not answering. There was a rustle, and then three pairs of well-shaved legs, all fragrant with spray tanner, were coming toward us. TR giggled, more than she needed to, playing up her double-edged friendliness. She was the de facto leader of the BRGs, alpha bitch, legend among Melva girls and guys alike ever since she'd supposedly shaved her crotch as an eighth-grader and flashed it for five high school guys during a game of truth or dare behind the Girl Scout hut in the city park. She and her pack surrounded us, looming above the table where we sat. Margo shivered beside me.

By remaining standing, thus maximizing their physical presence, the BRGs exert dominance over the weaker, lesser tribe.

"Hey, Margo, I don't think you heard me. Oh, hi, Janice," TR said, nodding at each of us. "I'm thinking of joining Science Club. Is it too late in the year?" She smirked at me.

"And you're entering Miss Livermush, right, Janice? Or will you have scientific obligations — excuse me, anthropological ones — that you need to attend to?" Tabitha added.

I hunched my shoulders in an awkward, nonresponsive shrug. Margo elbowed me, hissing, "We have to say something back! TR can't just do this!"

I shook my head. I was an anthropologist. An observer. Indeed, it was because of TR that I became an anthropologist in the first place. In seventh grade, I'd been stricken with the self-destructive urge to try out for middle school cheerleading. Yes, Janice Wills, Gangly McGangles, had wanted to be a *cheerleader*. Don't ask me from where this impulse had come, but with true monomaniacal madness, I'd been consumed with the desire to dance around and do splits and smile my face off. (I could not and cannot dance. I could not and cannot do splits. And I don't smile excessively. I am, generally speaking, not a performative person.) I blame this whole episode on temporary insanity.

Anyway, I'd sheepishly, eagerly shown up at tryouts. TR, the team captain, quickly nicknamed me "Stilts the Clown" and

"Wobbles" after I fell (more than once) during the routines. Needless to say, Stilts the Clown had not made the middle school cheerleading squad. When I'd found out and gone home crying (at my lapse in judgment and subsequent humiliation more than anything), my mom had said to me, "Oh, darling. Sometimes to make it through these years, you just have to step back. Become an anthropologist when you need to, you know? Observe the behaviors around you without taking it too personally. It's just adolescence, after all. . . ."

My mom had made what she thought was merely an offhand comment, but I clung to her advice. Thinking like this seemed to be the only way to make myself feel better. And so I'd gone to the library and checked out every book on anthropology I could find, and what I couldn't find, I ordered off the Internet: *Ethnography Through Thick and Thin, Coming of Age in Samoa, Local Knowledge, From Lucy to Language, Critical Anthropology Now* . . . Not all of it had made complete sense to me, but I loved feeling like an explorer somehow, even if it was in my own town. I felt safe that way. Intellectual. And it was completely interesting! That was the best part — I actually liked this stuff. Cheerleading, blech, be gone! I was better suited to being an anthropologist anyway.

Back in the present moment, TR smiled her acid smile. In response, my own mouth arranged itself into a jigsaw of doubt.

"So, Margo," TR continued. "We like your shirt sooooo much. Just wondering, where did you get it?"

Tabitha and Casey were laughing silently at us, swallowing little snickers. TR gave a careless toss of her shimmery blond hair and then leaned toward Casey and Tabitha, whispering. I heard Tabitha mutter "drug dealer" and "baby." Anyone who'd been in Melva longer than forty-eight hours would have known that these words related to various threads of gossip about Margo's family currently in circulation. I wasn't sure how the drug dealer rumor had started, but Margo's older sister, Becca, had just had a baby during the past year. Margo's sister wasn't married. This had caused a small stir.

"So are y'all comin' to the party this Friday?" Tabitha asked. Margo didn't answer, recrossing her legs.

ANTHROPOLOGIST'S NOTE:
In warding off the attacking tribe, members of the weaker tribe must avoid direct confrontation — even the direct gaze will be taken as a challenge. Members of a weaker tribe must play dead and wait for the aggressors' interest to wane. Thus we kept silent.

"I heard that *last* Friday night someone saw you with a guy," Casey said, directing her attention toward Margo.

TR made a coughing noise that sounded like "slut." Margo flicked her raised foot dangerously close to TR's ankles.

"Hey," Casey said to TR. "We should get that stuff from my house for the junior class party. And then go check and see if they got that dress for Miss Livermush in a small enough size for you."

They had lost interest in us. I thought we were in the clear at that point, but no — too late. Margo cleared her throat and hawked up an enormous wad of phlegm. It landed, glistening, on the grungy floor, only millimeters from TR's pretty foot in its wedge sandal.

ANTHROPOLOGIST'S NOTE:
In the solitary act of retaliatory aggression, a lone member of the weaker tribe has, in popular parlance, "gone maverick." Such an act could trigger an all-out battle or a more indirect attack, but either way, the repercussions will likely affect the entire weaker tribe, not just the lone aggressor. In other words, Margo's actions made me very, very nervous.

TR coughed, smoothed her new jean skirt, and sidestepped the glob with her long legs. "Ohmygod! Wait!" she said, in the same fake, drawling voice she used to charm the First Baptist Church ladies and sell yearbook ads. "I can't believe how forgetful I am!"

"What? What did you forget?" Casey asked, now looking puzzled.

TR nodded and cast her long, purpley lashes downward, then looked sorrowfully over toward Margo.

"I was thinking," TR said. "With Miss Livermush coming up, and your family having a new baby in the house, you might be a little tight on money. And I believe in competition, so I want you in the pageant. I might have a dress you can borrow." She smiled sweetly, as if bestowing a generous gift. But then she frowned. "But, oh! Oh, no, it would definitely be too small for you, I guess. . . . Maybe Trisha Young has one you could borrow? Just to help you financially?"

FACT:
Trisha Young was approximately the size of a baby elephant. TR also managed to make the word "financially" sound like something chronic and contagious.

"I'm only trying to help," TR added, very softly. "Because left to your own devices, Margo, you dress like a schizophrenic homeless woman."

TR's phrase zinged past us like an arrow. No one spoke.

"Come on, girls. Let's get out of here. It's slirting time!" TR sang. The others cheered. They stepped past our table and left, leaving a cloud of tuberoses and honey-vanilla where they'd stood.

ANTHROPOLOGIST'S NOTE:
"Slirting," an activity popular with the BRGs, is a neologism derived from "slumming" and "flirting." Participants go after socially undesirable males for sport, flirting with them, teasing them, leading them on, and

potentially even obtaining free drinks or other items from them, only to humiliate them ultimately. TR and her pals enjoyed targeting a hangout popular among guys from the county, because they felt that "slirting with rednecks" was a particularly thrilling way to reinforce their sneering superiority. (As an anthropologist, I try to record behaviors without moral commentary, but let it be known that I find "slirting" to be reprehensible and disgusting.)

"Well," I said when the door had closed behind them.

Margo released a pent-up growl. "I can't stand them!" Her fists were squeezed so tight they'd turned white, and I could see a pulse bound in her throat.

How much easier it was to be at an anthropologic remove, I insisted to myself. *Distance*, I thought. *Safe distance.*

"Margo," I said. "You've got to get a little more anthropological about this stuff. Step back, disengage from the enemy tribe. It's much safer."

Margo glared at me. She was still clenching her fists when I noticed a handsome college-aged guy walk in. He looked like he'd just stepped out of a college brochure in which everyone is reading contemplatively on grassy lawns or in the midst of an Ultimate Frisbee game. I turned my head down to avoid his glance.

Why avoid the gaze of handsome guys? His gaze was a trick, and I knew it. The guy was a FreshLife leader from the local

Baptist college. FreshLife is a fellowship group for high school students that tries to make God seem like your cousin's friend's hip, young Hollywood uncle and Jesus like some spring breaker gone wild — gone wild with praise, that is. If you were cool with Jesus, you were a VIP at the hottest spot in town. FreshLife seduced you with the handsome college-aged leaders and free beach trips. Then on Monday nights, you were expected to gather and sing songs to acoustic guitars and play weird, embarrassing games involving Cool Whip or egg tossing. I know because I'd gone before, at my mom's request, of course. They usually only threw in two minutes or so of God talk — it was just the manic games and singing I couldn't stand. And the retreats. The retreats were always to places like Myrtle Beach or Gatlinburg, and I'd heard they involved much candle holding and tearful soliloquies from otherwise viperish girls — BRGs included. Given the choice, I would rather read long genealogies out of the Bible for hours at a time. Forced friendliness freaked me out.

The college guy — Colin, I think his name was — looked at Margo and me. Colin was scruffy and, yes, really good-looking. For this reason, he was an extremely effective evangelical tool. The FreshLife attendance (at least the female portion) had surged this year, or so I'd heard. But rather than trying to recruit us, he turned quickly away and headed, scone in hand, out the door of the Mocha Cellar.

Margo gulped her iced tea.

"Hey, that was weird," I said. "That FreshLife guy totally saw us and pretended he didn't. FreshLife Leaders never avoid possible targets."

Margo shrugged. "Weird," she said.

"No, *totally* weird," I said. "I fully explored the aggressively friendly nature of the FreshLife Leader in 'Margaret Mead, Melva, and Me,' and my scientific conclusion was that they never miss an opportunity to proselytize."

Margo shrugged again. "Come on," she said. "I'm too restless to sit here. Let's walk around outside."

We walked to Melva's uptown, which features the old court square — our one, sad point of pride. The outskirts of Melva, the part of town along the highway, can be depressing — the fractured stoplights, the Kmart, an ugly hunk of mall, too many all-you-can-eat restaurants, and the ever-crowded Alston-Henry Barbecue. Of course, then you drive uptown, and things get a bit snobbier, or classier — depending on your view. There's the old banker's house, the M. Scott Werther mansion — one of the big, restored Victorian relics of the days when Margo's recent ancestors dominated state politics. Manicured women power walk their fluffy dogs by those graceful old porches and cupolas. The shops surrounding the court square sell handcrafted beaded jewelry from Charleston, sleek silver pens, and monogrammed linens from an Atlanta boutique. Two upscale restaurants with fresh flowers on every table serve sweet tea in cool blue glasses and herbed sweet potatoes. In this part of Melva, an old name is worth more than any amount of money — which is good, because recently, money has been in short supply.

For the majority of Melva, the two things that hold the most importance are 1) biscuits and 2) Wednesday night church supper. Trucks might be number three. Wrestling and high school football four and five. In other words, Melva is a town of biscuit-eating sports enthusiasts who smile, pray, and sing the national anthem while the town seems to be crumbling under everyone's feet.

"This court square's gotten to be so cheesy," I said, pointing to Kassie's Kozy Korner: A Kidz Shop! This is what passed for cuteness in Melva: alliterative misspellings.

"As opposed to?" Margo asked.

"I dunno," I said. "As opposed to nothing. I'm just sick of how nobody cares about anything outside of this place. No one has any interest in the world outside Melva. Everyone thinks Melva *is* the world." I gestured to the Confederate War Memorial plaque in the square. "That," I said. "That's the world. That's the extent of what anyone knows here. It's the court square and Miss Livermush and that's it. The end."

"But it gives you something to study, right?" Margo asked. "As an anthropologist?"

"Yeah," I said. "Nincompoops engaged in nincompoopery." But then I saw TR's wickedly pretty face smiling in my mind and had a flash of inspiration — the entire plan. It was too perfect. The surest way to get into *Current Anthropology* yet.

"I've got it!" I said, feeling my heart begin to pound a little more strongly. "You know what I have to do? I have to *enter* Miss Livermush after all."

Margo looked askance at me. "What? Seriously? Your mom's gonna weep with joy," she said. "But why the sudden change of heart?"

"I've got to see the pageant *from the inside*. I need to experience the perspective of an actual participant!" I practically yelped. "It's regional, it's quirky, it's perfect! Don't worry — I'm still gonna help you take down TR, but this is how I'm going to get my real material!"

It would be so easy: I could take notes on pageant preparations, read some Livermush Festival history for context, and then just observe. Now that I stopped to think about it, the whole thing was a research bonanza. This was my ticket into *Current Anthropology*.

Margo raised her eyebrows, then gave me a thumbs-up. "Yes!" she said. "It'll be so much better to have company!"

"Now," I said. "I was gonna tell you this earlier. Guess who walked up to me and started a conversation during lunch today?"

ANTHROPOLOGICAL
OBSERVATION #4:

Throughout high school, one must look good without looking like one is trying too hard to look good, as the appearance of effortless, semi-intentional beauty is highly prized among the adolescent species. This is impossible for most people to accomplish.

The rules of the Melva's Miss Livermush Pageant and Scholarship competition are as follows:

I. Contestants must be girls who are completing their junior year in Letherfordton County, at either Melva High School or the Letherfordton County High School.

2. Contestants must have and maintain a GPA of 3.4 or above. The judges evaluate each contestant's academic record and award academic points.

3. Contestants must be of "excellent moral character." (A purposefully vague guideline, yes, but useful in disqualifying girls for all manner of youthful indiscretions.)

4. Contestants must complete an essay on the topic "What Livermush Means to Me."

5. And, most important, the final twenty contestants must compete onstage (humiliatingly!) at the annual Livermush Festival. Each must wear a fancy dress and perform a talent (often stupid), then answer a question (dumbly) during the interview portion of the competition.

There was one more guideline that you wouldn't see on the official rules: Although the contest was technically open to anyone, the contest participants were invariably, monochromatically white. This added to the pageant's overarching antebellum nostalgia. There was a similar pageant sponsored by the Association of Black Civic Leaders that tended to attract any girl of non-Euro ancestry.

If you meet those requirements, as I've said before, there is basically no getting out of the Miss Livermush Pageant. You *have* to participate. Or else. You're out. Off the island. People would stop inviting you to Sunday lunch at the Country Buffet after church, and you wouldn't get monogrammed towels from the neighbor ladies as your high school graduation presents. There'd be no invitation to the post–Miss Livermush mother-daughter tea waiting in your mailbox. Which was why my mom was so horrified at the mere idea of my refusal to participate.

There was also the Livermush Festival Dance afterward, which basically everyone in Melva age sixteen and above attended, moms and dads and grandmas and all. It was the community's time to see and be seen, and that's why it was such a big deal.

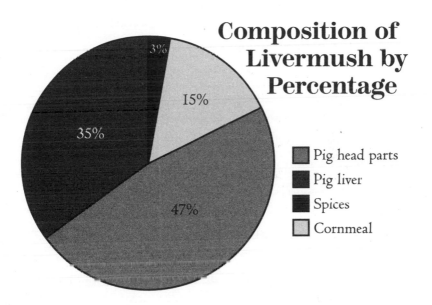

Composition of Livermush by Percentage

- Pig head parts
- Pig liver
- Spices
- Cornmeal

3%

15%

35%

47%

ANTHROPOLOGIST'S NOTE:

Melva, North Carolina, has long been known as the Livermush Capital of the World. Livermush is a traditional Southern favorite — a meat product made of pig liver and head parts (mmm, right?), cornmeal, and spices. To celebrate this culinary tradition, every spring for decades Melva has held the Livermush Festival uptown. (I always forget that often outside of Melva, and definitely outside of North Carolina, people have never heard of livermush.)

Now that I'd decided to get the inside view of Miss Livermush, I was contemplating my strategy while watching the E! entertainment channel evening news roundup. The E! channel was my major televised source for pop cultural information (a trick I'd picked up from Margo), and it gave me some good topics to discuss with my non-anthropology-minded peers.

FACT:
Most of the other kids at MHS only knew of the existence of other countries if Angelina Jolie had adopted a baby from them.

So, I thought strategy. I definitely needed a performable Miss Livermush talent, and I had zero performable talents. The talents I possessed were best practiced in libraries, not on stages. The academic portion of the competition was my only real competitive edge. The judges evaluated your livermush essay, your GPA — but even so, everyone knew that a pretty girl won each year!

Grabbing a handful of sugary cereal from the box open at my feet, I crunched, turning my attention back to E!. Clips of celebrities in formal gowns flickered across the screen. Periodically, the host would offer commentary, her breasts bobbing treacherously like floatie devices.

ANTHROPOLOGIST'S NOTE:
The ancient Greeks linked breasts with distinctly feminine divine powers. But they also told stories of Amazon

women who cut off their right breasts to better draw back their bows. At Melva High School, breasts were merely associated with "hotness," "sluttiness," and whether you wanted to "hit that" — at least according to what I'd overheard in hallway conversations of the masculine variety.

It occurred to me that whoever won Miss Livermush actually had it pretty good — there was scholarship money at stake. A lot of scholarship money. Winning a scholarship could change my whole life plan. I'd been thinking about applying to colleges I'd heard had particularly good anthropology departments — Harvard, Michigan, UC Berkeley, or even the University of Arizona (where Dr. Aldenderfer taught). But then my mom said, "Arizona? That's a great school — great for people who live in Arizona, but you know it's much more expensive because we're out of state. And I'm sure that the UNC and NC State anthropology departments are excellent!"

So I was going to apply to the University of North Carolina– Chapel Hill in the fall. Maybe I would find a good excuse to email the anthropology faculty ahead of time. ("Dear Dr. So and So, I am an incoming freshman. Please be on the lookout for my forthcoming articles on American adolescence in *Current Anthropology.* . . .")

But maybe if I had some extra scholarship money, I could apply to those other schools too. Go far, far away from Melva — far from the North Carolina state line. Maybe I'd end up the undergraduate anthro star at Berkeley. Or maybe Arizona was exactly the place I'd fit in. There, in the circle of the intelligentsia, I'd become non-awkward and beautiful. I'd befriend all the anthropology professors and grad students. Guys would abound who said things like, "My dream girl would definitely skip cool parties in order to rewatch DVDs of *The Wire* and National Geographic documentaries," and "Subtitles?! I LOVE subtitles!" I paused for a minute, almost forgetting the Miss Livermush entry form in my hand.

I also needed a Miss Livermush escort. Didn't I? Although escorts were not required, it seemed most girls chose to have one. Escorts had no clear-cut role in the pageant itself, but they were listed in the program and counted as your date for the dance afterward. So in that way, it was a big deal: Your date was publicly announced. I saw Jimmy Denton standing before me in his dark jeans and T-shirt. . . . No, no, no, no. Not even a possibility.

Then I thought of Paul. Paul might have been willing, but what about The Girlfriend? She'd probably want him to escort her. I didn't really understand Paul anyway, and apparently never had. There had been the humiliating incident of the Disastrous Almost-Kiss — an incident that had utterly confused me, an incident on which I did not like to speculate because it was too embarrassing, an incident I hadn't mentioned, even to Margo, because I couldn't tell if I'd just wildly misread the whole situation. It had happened last year, before The Girlfriend came along.

THE DISASTROUS ALMOST-KISS (????)

One weekend Paul and I had gone to his house to eat burritos and watch an old movie. This was not atypical — at least it had not been before The Girlfriend came along in all her legitimate girlfriendness. And that night, it had almost seemed like something might happen, something more than the same old Gal Pal Janice story. I wasn't sure what to think about it because the possibility felt so strange — Paul, my friend, as Paul, my boyfriend? I had never consciously thought about him that way, at least not prior to that evening. Maybe it was that he'd complimented my hair that evening. Maybe it had been the way his mom had jokingly winked at us before we'd started the movie. But I have to admit, at least that particular night, the hint of whatever in the air, the tension between us — well, it was exciting. I'd felt trembly in my throat the whole night. When our hands had accidentally brushed over the salsa, Paul had blushed and recoiled as if burned. And when the movie had finally ended, we'd both sat there silently, watching the blank screen and listening to only a faint electronic whirring. The lights were out, and we were motionless, neither daring to turn on the light nor to face the other.

Finally Paul had said, a little too loudly, "Janice." I'd turned in the darkness to face him. As if drawn by a force unseen, our faces had moved closer together. The tips of our noses were almost touching. In the movies, I knew that the kissers always closed their eyes, but mine were wide-open. I was so close to

Paul's face that if it hadn't been dark, I could have seen his pores. Then, suddenly and startlingly, Paul jumped up.

"Shoot! I forgot to feed Barker. I haven't fed him at all today!"

Barker was the Hansen family's ancient golden retriever. I liked Barker. I didn't want him to starve to death. But as I watched Paul flip on the lights and slip out of the room, I felt a growing horror. The guy I'd been about to kiss had leapt to his feet to feed his dog. This could only mean a couple things, both of them bad: Either he realized that he desperately did NOT want to kiss me and could figure no other way out of the situation, or he actually DID realize that he needed to feed Barker, meaning that he'd been thinking of his pet dog just as he was about to kiss me. I didn't know which possibility was worse.

When Paul had come back from feeding Barker, he was whistling. He bent down to the DVD player and pressed EJECT, removing the disc and popping it back into the case.

"Boy, Barker's never been so happy to see me. Poor old guy, he was starving."

Still seated on the floor, I'd nodded, looked at my watch, then said I needed to get going. And that night, lying in bed, my whole face had burned in humiliation — so hot that I thought the pillow would ignite. I'd then avoided Paul for a while, and he started dating The Girlfriend, and the whole incident of the Almost-Kiss had never come up.

Maybe, I thought now, he hadn't been planning to kiss me at all — maybe he'd actually just been practicing meditation. Maybe he was a narcoleptic. Maybe the whole Almost-ness of the Almost-Kiss was a figment of my idiot imagination. Maybe I had no insight into patterns of adolescent male behavior at all.

A knocking at the front door broke my reverie. I looked at my watch. It was almost 9 p.m., a strange time for anyone to show up at our front door. I rose to go see who it was and met my mom in the hallway.

"Are you expecting someone?" she asked. I shook my head.

On opening the door, there stood Margo — or the person formerly known as Margo. I stared at her, and she stared back at me. We said nothing. This new person had hair that had been carefully straightened and highlighted, unlike Margo's hair, which was normally a mass of wild curls. She wore tasteful makeup — mascara, just a hint of blush, lip gloss. Her finger-nails were impeccably manicured — true, in a color that I'd most often seen on loudmouthed girls named Misti Krystal or Gennyfer Tammi-Ann — but still! And her shirt, it was soft and formfitting and —

"Ralph Lauren?!" my mom exhaled, unable to help herself. You had to drive to Charlotte to get clothes like that, and my mom, I knew, secretly imagined herself to be a fancier person — the sort of person who drove to Charlotte regularly for Ralph Lauren — although she would never fully admit to this vanity. She salivated over brand names and couldn't help invoking them whenever possible. In this way, my mom was not unlike a rap video.

"You like?" Margo asked, giving us a twirl. She was flushed

and looked a) older b) happier c) innocently eager for approval d) pretty. Really, really, teeth-clenchingly pretty.

"Wow," my mom said. "Margo, you look great. Like someone from a makeover show."

"I'm not sure that's a compliment, Mom."

"She knows what I mean, don't you, dear?" my mom said — my mom, who is a great fan of makeover shows and anything else with a "before" and "after" image. "And it's very much a compliment."

Margo nodded. "You two really like?" she asked, eyeing the lovely architecture of her own ankles as she arched and flexed in the new kitten-heeled sandals she wore.

My mom and I nodded, still staring at her. She was experiencing all the benefits of The Cinderella Effect. The transformation. I should confess that I felt a familiar feeling creeping up into my throat, a feeling perhaps best labeled "jealousy." I nudged my mom, and she gave New and Improved Margo a little hug, waved to us both, and then went back upstairs.

"Margo, what happened?" I whispered now that it was just us. I thought about TR's schizophrenic-homeless-woman comment earlier in the day — but no, surely that wasn't it. TR said stuff like that all the time.

"I needed a change," Margo said. "I figured, Janice, if you're going to work on your seeing-the-pageant-from-the-inside anthropology project, then I need to work on something too — like maybe actually putting some effort into the pageant, just to see if I could place, you know? I've been working on a solo part for the next chorus concert anyway . . . and I could really use the scholarship money. So I told my mom I was gonna try to 'look more presentable,' as she calls it, and she let me borrow her credit card. And I was kinda sick of wearing those ugly clothes. Becca's old shirts and stinky thrift store pants and whatever."

I returned to speechlessness, staring. It was great. Great for Margo. Not my style exactly, but it was the transformation I envied — a transformation I might secretly write into the movie version of my own life: *Janice Wills: Story of a Young Anthropologist*.

I think Margo realized I was mesmerized by her new appearance.

"Uh, I could help you too, Janice," she said. "I mean, I know it's not really your thing or whatever, but since we're both gonna do Miss Livermush now . . . It's not really that hard, with just a little makeup in the right colors and —"

"Thanks, but no thanks," I said. It's less humiliating to fail at looking pretty when you weren't trying to look pretty in the first place. Easier and safer not to try. "I keep it scientific. Dian Fossey didn't need mascara when she was out studying gorillas. That's how I roll."

During my brief Dian Fossey obsession, I'd made Margo watch *Gorillas in the Mist* with me four times in a matter of weeks. "Um, okay," Margo said. "But isn't that a weird reference since Dian Fossey got macheted by poachers, and she was studying gorillas, not people?"

I wasn't sure how to answer. So instead, I said, "Wow. You know TR's going to freak out, right? She's going to realize that you're serious competition."

She smiled slightly, shrugging.

"Wait a second," I said. "Does this have something to do with Secret Boyfriend?"

Margo examined the toe of one of her dainty new shoes without answering me. I kept staring at her, waiting for her to look up. Secret Boyfriend was the lone element of tension between Margo and me. Basically she had a Secret Boyfriend but didn't want to tell me about him. It was weird because a) neither of us had really ever had boyfriends prior to this and b) neither of us had really ever had secrets prior to this. If I'd had a boyfriend, I certainly would have told her. (Heck, I would have told everyone, while of course pretending that I wasn't. Like, my boyfriend would be in an awesome band, and I'd wear the band T-shirt all the time, and then people would ask about it, and I'd say, "Oh, this? Yeah, it's my boyfriend's band." You get the idea.) Margo apparently handled things a little differently, resulting in the mystery that was Secret Boyfriend.

Finally Margo looked up at me. She inhaled deeply. "Janice, I promise," she said. "It's not a big deal. We've barely hung out at this point, and I want to tell you — really I do. But I promised not to — it's just . . . He's asked me not to tell people yet. I trust you, I do, but . . . I promised him, and he's not even Secret Boyfriend yet, you know? He's more like Secret We've-Hung-Out-Twice Friend at this point anyway. . . ."

I could tell from Margo's face that she felt bad, and I felt bad making her feel bad — so there was just a lot of badness hovering around us.

"It's okay," I said. "I don't get it, but I understand you made a promise." I hugged her. "And hey, your new look is beautiful. TR's eyes are going to bug out of her head." Even though I smiled my It's-No-Big-Deal! smile at her as I said it, I felt sad and left out. And even as she stood there, I felt Margo was slipping away from me.

ANTHROPOLOGICAL OBSERVATION #5:

The more handsome the individual, the higher his social caste; the higher the social caste, the more awkward you will become if he is inviting you to a party, thereby lowering the odds of any future party invitations. And thus the high school social caste system is more or less maintained.

At school the next day, everyone was talking about Margo. New and Improved Margo, that is.

"Last week she was, like, totally Trailer Park Sue," I overheard one senior girl standing near my locker say to her friend, "and this week Margo Werther's, like, megacute!"

I guessed Margo was used to people whispering about her, thanks to her family and perceived Bad Girl Potential and all, but this was a different kind of whispering. So far, I hadn't asked her about it. My quietness was either tact or confusion. It was like Margo was morphing before my eyes into someone else, someone I barely knew — a polished, glamorous stranger with secrets she couldn't tell me.

On Thursdays, Margo and I had the same lunch period. Often our sort-of friend Missy Wheeler joined us. (I thought of her as "the Third Wheeler.") "Look!" Missy pointed with a carrot taken from her plastic baggie. "They're doing it again! That group of senior guys is totally checking Margo out. Don't look, but they keep turning this way."

Margo pinkened. I peeked at them. *Were* they looking at Margo? It was tough to tell. This particular group of guys — Future Business Golfers — wore a rotating array of pastel collared shirts and expensive sunglasses so I couldn't actually make out their eyes.

"Hey! Margo!"

It was Theresa Rose. I turned, my fight-or-flight system revving into gear. After a pause, I realized TR wasn't planning on greeting me as well. She'd walked right up to the table, looking directly at Margo.

"Hey. What's up?" Margo said, narrowing her eyes suspiciously, but still cool and polite.

"Your hair looks really good, Margo," TR said. "Your whole look. It's, well — it's great."

TR actually sounded completely sincere, something I'd never heard before. There wasn't a trace of sarcasm in her voice. I studied her face, looking for signs of latent mockery. Nothing. She almost looked nervous.

"Thanks, TR," Margo said. "That's really nice of you to say."

"Yeah," she said. "You'll have to take me to your hairstylist sometime. I need a new one. Anyway. Later." And with that, TR walked away.

"What was that about?" I hissed. "Totally devious. Something's up."

Margo stirred her yogurt thoughtfully while I ripped into my sandwich.

"Next thing you know, TR will have you all dolled up so you can go 'slirting' for some poor guy in a John Deere hat. Despicable," I said, almost spitting the word. I was about to elaborate further on the Perils of a Suddenly Nice (or *Seemingly Nice*) TR when another person approached.

"Hi, Janice."

I almost choked on my hunk of sandwich. It was Jimmy Denton.

We all turned toward his deep, quiet voice. He was standing behind Margo, so close to her that I could imagine the heat of his body radiating down her back. My mouth hung open, half-chewed sandwich on display. I shut it. Margo, Missy, and I stared up at him.

"Hi," I said.

"Hi," Margo said.

"How's it going?" Jimmy asked, nodding first at Margo, then me. He paused, shifty-eyed, his voice a low rumble. "My buddies and I are having a party tomorrow and wanted to invite you."

Margo shifted, craning her neck to face him. Missy and I remained frozen.

"Could be a research opportunity for you, Janice," Jimmy said. "Although maybe it's best to leave any notes at home this time." He winked at me as he said this.

(Jimmy Denton shared a private joke with me?! And winked at me?? I had officially entered an alternate reality.)

"Uh, yeah," I said. "Sounds great. We'll try and make it."

Jimmy nodded and walked away.

Missy exhaled loudly. Her face was red, and her eyes were huge. I swallowed the slobbery chunk of sandwich that had been dissolving in my mouth.

"Oh. My. God. He's so into one of us. He is such a depressive weirdo, but he's, like, madly in love with one of us," Missy said, her words spilling quickly. "Oh, wow, he's handsome. But he drinks a lot, you know? That's what I heard. And seems, like, so completely depressed? But hot, at least in a weird, potential-felon kinda way."

I felt a warmth rising again in my neck and cheeks and almost pointed out to Missy that Jimmy hadn't seemed aware of *her* presence at all, and that I didn't think his "weird, potential-felon" invitation extended to her anyway, but I bit my tongue. And then I reminded myself that Jimmy was just being friendly. I mustn't raise false hopes for myself. And who was I kidding — Jimmy was the Mount Everest of Coolness and I was like this inconspicuous ant. . . .

"We should go to the party," Missy continued breathlessly, her attention focused on Margo, not me. "I think he's into you, Margo! Everyone's noticing you today! He stood so close. Jimmy's gotta be totally into you!"

Margo looked away from Missy and toward me. I was fiddling with my sandwich, pulling it apart.

"Whatever," she said. "He was completely macking and attacking on Janice here."

"You're crazy," I mumbled, further dismantling my sandwich. It was more humiliating now that Margo felt the need to protect me, to feel sorry for me.

"No, seriously," Margo continued. "He's, like, *connected* to you. You're simpatico — soul mates, you know? He's completely into your anthropology research."

I smiled at Margo. She always knew the right thing to say.

"Hey, speaking of guys, who's this guy I hear you've been hanging out with, Margo?" Missy asked.

So, other people knew, I thought. I wasn't the only one who'd figured out that Margo was seeing some guy. Margo poked at her Tater Tots before responding.

"I don't even know what you're talking about," she said coolly. "Sure, I get lots of different calls from lots of different people. I had a friend for a while, a male friend. But nothing's come of it. He doesn't even go to MHS."

And Margo, pressing her lips together, gave us a look. The subject was finished, and we knew not to challenge her. It didn't take an anthropologist or a mind reader, however, to sense that Margo was lying. Secret Boyfriend, whoever he was, would remain a secret for now.

Meanwhile, the spot where Jimmy Denton had been standing fizzled with electric energy. I imagined him touching the small of my back, and the hot ghost-imprint of his imagined hand tingled there. I took another bite of my sandwich and reminded myself that I had the cool, observational mind of a researcher.

(But seriously — Jimmy Denton had just invited me, specifically, to a party??!!?!)

Paul walked by with a stack of posters. He and the new kid, Shaan, taped a few on the wall near the lunch line. They walked back toward us.

"What's up, guys?" Margo asked.

"Hey," Paul said. "We're just putting up some posters for the new Muslim Student Alliance. First meeting next Tuesday."

"Are there even any Muslims *in* Melva?" Missy asked.

Paul didn't quite look at Shaan, and Shaan coughed a little bit. I think his family was originally from Pakistan.

"Uh, well, you're right — there aren't that many," Paul said. "Which makes it all the more important that we support dialogue and awareness. And the alliance is open to Muslims and non-Muslims — anyone who's interested in learning more about Islam and Islamic culture."

Shaan smiled at Paul appreciatively. "Well, we've got a lot more signs to put up," he said, and the two left. I watched them go, a little wistful of their sense of purpose.

"What a flake," Missy said. "It's like each day he's all about something new."

"Jeez, Missy," I said.

"What? You're allowed to say stuff about everyone and call it 'anthropology' while nobody else can?" Missy responded.

"Well," Margo said, "Paul's either a flake or the most thoughtful guy in town."

The Future Business Golfers burst out laughing at some hilarious joke. Casting my eyes in their direction, I saw TR doing a silly little pirouette. She smirked at me, and I reminded myself that I'd once smelled TR's feet in the locker room, and they smelled like rotting carcasses. I made a mental note to include this piece of information in my anthropological data.

ANTHROPOLOGICAL OBSERVATION #6:

Dancing is a polarizing social behavior among adolescents — individuals either love it or loathe it. Some view it as wonderful "fun," while others (this investigator included) think of it as akin to public torture.

If I had a nickel for every time I'd been asked out on a legitimate date, I'd have zero cents. Well, correction, five cents — there had been the Petey Bivins incident. If that counted.

Petey was enormously fat and smelled like 2 percent milk. He was also smart, and occasionally hilarious. I'd always enjoyed his presence from a distance. The day he asked me out, though, I'd figured something was wrong, because he kept edging close and then backing away from me like a stray cat. Finally, at the end of our English class, he leaned in toward me. So close that I smelled the milk on his breath, the baby-powdery scent of his hair, the sour spittle on his quadruple chin. This was not, I thought, how a grown man should smell.

"I was wondering, Janice," he said, fumbling his pockets, "if you'd be into these dancing lessons my mom's harassing me about. It's, like, some friend of hers who's teaching partnered dances at the Y, and, like, it'd just be a favor . . . and, well, I just remembered how at cotillion in middle school we always won the dance contest."

FACT:

Junior cotillion is an organized class that attempts to teach young people social graces and manners through formal dance. It's practically obligatory here in Melva — nearly every middle school parent signs his or her child up. So, just when you are at your most awkward, you get to stumble through old-fashioned dance steps with some snickering middle school boy who probably doesn't want to be dancing with you either.

But what Petey said was true. Petey and I, like all good seventh and eighth graders in our town, had attended Mrs. James Biddlesworth's junior cotillion. Every other Saturday night, we'd gathered in the Episcopal church basement and danced to songs like "Up on the Roof" and "I Love Beach Music." We learned basic box steps, the waltz, and Carolina beach dances like the shag. No one was allowed to decline when asked to dance, which I found to be a real relief — although I loudly complained about this rule along with everyone else.

"Dancing with someone with whom you'd rather not builds character. Do not decline a request to dance. This is how we become polite members of society," Mrs. Biddlesworth always said.

Then, in December and again in May, there were two big events: the Holly Ball and the Spring Ball. Everyone wore formal dresses and tuxedos. There was a dance contest too, and Petey and I had been, believe it or not, the reigning champions. I remembered his sweaty hands in mine, the forced gaiety of the music, my stumbling hesitations, the clunky clodhopper flats my mom had gotten dyed to match my gown because I had refused any shoe that would have made me taller than I already was. Song after song played, and Mrs. Biddlesworth and her assistants tapped other couples, notifying them that they were out and must leave the floor. Song after song, and Petey and I stayed on the floor.

Petey's face was red, sweating. His soft, billowing belly belonged to a middle-aged man, not a seventh grader, but he moved gracefully, lightly on the polished wood floor. Whenever I stumbled or skipped a step, Petey gently guided me back. He was actually a pretty good lead. When we'd won, I'd secretly been pleased. Mrs. James Biddlesworth (supposedly drunk by that time in the evening from a secret flask it was rumored she kept tucked in her cleavage) had raised our hands like we were boxing champions and awarded us prizes. The prize had been candy cane earrings (for me) and McDonald's gift certificates (for both of us). We stayed partners for all the cotillion dance contests after that, and won all but one.

Only later had it occurred to me that maybe the reason Petey and I had usually won had less to do with the quality of our dancing than the judges' pity. A puffy kid and a solemn, gangly tall girl whose big glasses kept fogging up with perspiration: I imagined the adults had seen us, all concentration and seriousness, a ridiculous sight, and wanted to reward our earnest effort; and I had crushed my four sets of holiday-themed prize earrings in the trash compactor. Petey, on the other hand, apparently still believed we were destined for *So You Think You Can Dance*.

"I dunno, Petey," I'd said, after having paused to think. "I mean, I'd love to dance with you, but it's just . . . It's my schedule, really."

Petey had reddened a little. He drew an invisible line on the floor with his big, dorky basketball shoe.

"No, totally. Dumb idea. I understand," he said. "Forget I mentioned it. Hey, are you still working on your various anthropology projects?"

I nodded, flattered. Hardly anyone (until Jimmy recently) asked about my projects, and Petey had acted like it wasn't at least slightly weird.

"I'm trying. I'm probably going to focus on another topic here in Melva, actually," I said, "just because I can't afford Peru or New Zealand right now. And truthfully, it's mostly still inside my head. Thinking about it," I added, feeling like I should be realistic with Petey about the amount of work that I'd done at that point.

"Cool. I wanna read the latest when you're done."

And with that, Petey had turned and left. He continued to be nice to me after that too, but I've always felt terrible. Maybe I deserved loneliness for being too embarrassed to take Y dance classes with a very nice, hilarious fat boy.

ANTHROPOLOGIST'S NOTE:
Dance may have originated as part of storytelling or the performance of myths, or, in some cases, as part of early

healing rituals. I, for one, wish it would go back to being those things rather than being a major component of adolescent social life.

My mom, however, did not realize that I'd cursed my dating karma by turning down Petey two months before. And so she could afford to be cheerful about my romantic prospects, and she had been. Ever since I'd told her that I would be participating in Miss Livermush, she'd been the Escort Brainstorming Queen.

It was Friday morning, and my mom sometimes made oatmeal for my family on Fridays. When I got to the table, my brothers were already gobbling it down like small, hungry badgers. My mom was wearing her apron that read "I'm Da Boss," dancing to the radio, and lip-synching into a big wooden spoon. My dad ate his oatmeal quietly, paging through the business section of the Charlotte paper.

"*Hey, hey,*" sang my mom along with the song, "*hey, hey, Janice!* Oh, I have news for you! I talked to Robin Healey after Garden Club, and she said Chuck isn't escorting anyone in the Miss Livermush Pageant. I happened to mention to her that you didn't yet have an escort!"

I was stunned into momentary silence. Chuck Healey? Chuck?!

FACT:
Chuck still had braces and often wore his headgear to school. I once wore braces too, so I wouldn't hold this

against him, except he always had Snickers bars coating his teeth as well. Chuck liked aliens, and he thought wearing his headgear more often made him look more extraterrestrial. He also started the Manga Club at high school and preferred to go by Daisuke, "his Japanese name."

ADDITIONAL FACT:
I had a specific distaste for the Manga Club, since it was a direct rival to Science Club. We shared the same advisor and had an overlapping membership.

"Mom!" I cried. "No! I can't go with Chuck!"

"He's such a sweet boy, Janice. And so intellectually curious."

"He's an anime freak. He makes all the teachers call him 'Daisuke.'"

"Don't be cruel, Janice," my dad murmured, looking up at me above his reading glasses.

"He's a questing intellect!" my mom insisted.

I groaned, lifting a great spoonful of oatmeal and then letting it plop back into the bowl. I thought about Jimmy Denton. If we were of the same caste in India, maybe our parents would arrange for us to be married. So much less hassle! No work on my part! Arranged marriage seemed to make a lot of sense. Just leave it up to good ol' Mom and Dad. No humiliation, no rejection, no cute drama boys not knowing of your existence . . .

But you'd have to trust your parents' taste, which I did not. Having seen my mom's picks (and clearly, my mom would be the one doing the choosing), I most DEFINITELY would not leave a decision of such magnitude up to her.

"Well, there's always Paul Hansen," my mom said. "Y'all have known each other since you were babies, but you've refused that suggestion so many times. . . . I'm sticking with Chuck as my new nomination to become your boyfriend!"

"Paul has a girlfriend, and there's no way on earth I'm going near Chuck Healey."

"Janice loves Chuck Healey!" my brother Rufus sang.

"Janice and Chuck, ooh la la!" sang my other little brother, Simon.

"Just talk to him at school today, honey, and see what you two think," my mom said.

I looked at the bowl of oatmeal and considered dropping my face into it.

The phone rang, and my mom answered. "For you, Jan," she said, accidentally getting an oatmeal glob on the phone as she passed it over.

"Hello?"

"J, it's Paul. Bagels on the way to school? I can pick you up in ten."

"Yes, please! I'll be outside."

I hung up, jumped up from my chair (abandoning my uneaten oatmeal), and grabbed my bag. "I'm catching a ride with Paul, Mom. Bye! Bye, Dad!"

As I ran to get my history book from upstairs, I could still hear Rufus and Simon singing a nonsensical "Janice and Chuck" song they'd made up to the tune of "Santa Claus Is Coming to Town." My mom joined them, harmonizing, *You'd better watch out, you'd better not cry, Janice and Chuck, Janice and Chuck!"*

It didn't matter. I loved getting breakfast with Paul, even though it happened less often since I'd been demoted to second-place gal pal after The Girlfriend (who, being a musical theatre star, *of course* happened to be an excellent dancer and singer, the universe having a wicked sense of humor).

"Hey, Paul," I said when he showed up and I'd opened the car door. I smelled the faint mixture of his coconut shampoo and piney deodorant. My heart jumped up in my chest like it'd hit a speed bump. This did not ordinarily happen when I talked to Paul. It was just Paul.

"Hey, J. Ready to carbo-load?"

I nodded and hopped in beside him.

"So I have to admit it," he said as we pulled away. "Your most recent mix CD was pretty excellent. You've set the bar even higher. I'm not sure what I'm going to find in response. . . ."

"It's hard to compete with early Afrobeat mixed with some of the greatest hits coming out of 1961 Detroit, I know. . . ."

"I'll triumph, though. You're going to be dazzled, Janice. Oh, and I really liked the South African song you put on there." He gestured to his CD player.

I inhaled the familiar scent of Paul's car. It smelled like him — the shampoo and deodorant — plus coffee. There were pita chips and splashes of now-dried coffee seeped into the upholstery. Paul had a thing for eating while driving.

"So," he said, "what's the plan this evening?"

"Well, I think Margo and I might be going to that party that Jimmy Denton and some of the other senior drama guys are having."

Paul kept his eyes forward and nodded, but I could see a frown deepening the crease in his forehead.

"What, *Dad*, you don't approve?"

He sighed, shaking his head. We were at a stoplight, so he turned to face me. "No, I think Jimmy's fine, it's just . . . I heard he's been in a bad mood lately. He just has some issues he's working through, that's all. . . ."

ANTHROPOLOGIST'S NOTE:

"Issues"? Issues! This had definitely become the most vague and yet one of the most frequently used terms of my generation.

"Besides," Paul added, "a bunch of us were talking about going to the movies tonight. You interested?"

I shrugged. I figured The Girlfriend would surely be there, and the thought of going to the movies with perfect, porcelain Susannah was almost as appealing as looking for extraterrestrial life-forms with Chuck Healey.

As if he weren't thinking about it, Paul put his hand on my forearm. With the too-bright sun pouring in through the car windows and his fingers on my skin, I felt time slow down. He was touching my arm, and his hand was radiant with warmth like a miniature sun. He crinkled his crinkly brown eyes at me. Kind eyes. He worried about me! And I loved his hand on my arm.

ANTHROPOLOGIST'S NOTE:
There is an interesting tradition of belief in the power of the "healing touch." It involves various energies that I don't really understand. I'd previously thought this idea sounded funny and quaint, but whatever was radiating from Paul's hand, I was becoming a believer.

Then he took his hand away. The elastic stretch of the moment snapped back, and we were back in the sickly coffee-smelling car, and the stoplight was changing, and there was no more touching, and — oh, God — I realized why his hand had jerked back — oh, God — repulsed.

The Mutant Hair.

There, in the unforgiving natural light, I saw it. The Mutant Hair spiraled annoyingly out of one juicy brown mole on my left arm. It was glistening and dark, whereas the rest of my arm was downed lightly with blond. It was a man's hair, a weird pubic sprout coiling from that cursed mole. Normally I kept track of The Mutant Hair and jerked it from its mole as soon as it was long enough, but I'd been forgetful. Now Paul had seen it and surely thought I was disgusting. Repulsive. A manly ogre. Only he was too polite to say so.

"Thanks, Paul. A movie sounds good, but I already talked about the party with Margo. Maybe next time?" I said it cheerily, as if nothing odd had happened, but my stomach sank like I'd gone down a huge roller coaster.

"Sure, next time," he said lightly. "There's probably more for a young anthropologist to behold at Jimmy's party anyway."

I nodded, cradling my arm awkwardly on my lap so as to hide The Mutant Hair, silently vowing to retreat into hermitude as soon as possible: Janice Wills, the secular anthropologist-nun.

We parked outside the Melva Bagel Shop, but before we could get out of the car, he looked at me, a little shyly.

"I've missed seeing you," he said. "I've missed talking to you. I realized that after we ran into each other during lunch the other day."

I swallowed and simply nodded.

Paul looked even more embarrassed. This, for some reason, made me feel slightly better.

"Did you make a decision about the Miss Livermush Pageant?" He forced a little laugh. "And the lucky gentleman who will be your escort?"

When he asked this, I imagined Susannah, The Lovely Victorian, winning Melva's Miss Livermush. I saw her being escorted by a Victorian Paul in a top hat. This image made me want to vomit — and I am ordinarily a fan of top hats.

"Oh, I'm participating," I said. "It'll be my greatest research yet. But as for an escort, it's been hard to decide. All the handsomest gentlemen in the land have been vying for my affection. They fell in love with my beauty, charm, and Miss Livermush grace — just like they always do. I'll have to pick my winning escort soon, but there may be a few duels first, with all these guys fighting over my favor." I sighed. "Yeah, right."

"Janice, you're always so hard on people . . . yourself included," Paul said, looking kindly but steadily into my eyes.

"It's the way the world works," I said, exasperated with him.

He shook his head. "Not for everybody. Here, I made you this. It's just sort of a joke, but I thought you might enjoy it," he said, handing me a typed sheet of paper. This is what it said:

    Anthropological Observations of Janice Wills
                   by Paul Hansen

1. The Janice Wills creature is of slight, birdlike
    frame and can be found in her natural habitat
    around the environs of Melva, NC.

2. She can be recognized by the anthropology book in
    her hand — if she has a freshman anthropology
    textbook from any university, then she is not
    Janice (the actual Janice read all the major
    introductory texts years ago).

3. Her aesthetic is nerd-chic-hipster, still in the
    formative and slightly fumbling years.

4. She tends to be more comfortable keeping to the
    fringe of things, watching others and making
    observations.

5. She is hypercritical, so while in her presence, please do not discuss Renaissance festivals or role-playing games, snort while laughing, or do anything else that she might deem unbecoming. At the very least, aim for sarcasm/irony. Also, best not to have eaten cheese puffs immediately before seeing her.

I stopped reading, letting the paper drop from my hand.

"You think I don't participate, I just watch. You think I'm hypercritical," I said. My eyes were watering.

"Janice, I was just teasing. I thought you'd think it was funny — you know, a little anthropology report on you, I —"

"No, it's not a big deal," I said, feeling stupid and terrible. "I don't even care."

Susannah, the beautiful Victorian, was probably incapable of observing anyone's flaws. To her, Stephen Shepherd's breath probably smelled like damask roses.

He picked the sheet of paper up, eyeing it uncertainly.

"You're not going to finish it?" he asked. "I think you'd like the rest more."

"No," I said, fearing that I might break into full tears, "another time. I'm sure it's funny."

"Well," Paul said, frowning as he folded the paper and tucked it into his pocket. "I also wanted to talk to you about your plans. . . . Susannah and I —"

"I don't care what you and Susannah are doing. Y'all have fun being artistic and pure and kind. You and Susannah just have a blast." Now I was definitely on the brink of crying, but I didn't want to look any stupider in front of him. So I got out of the car and walked. I walked the rest of the way to school, and my stomach ached with either a very specific, gnawing hunger for bagels, or else just plain humiliation.

ANTHROPOLOGICAL OBSERVATION #7:

Instead of cowrie shells, beauty and social prominence are the two most important forms of currency in high school hallways.

When fourth period ended, I felt a burst of, if not joy, relief. I'd been thinking about my encounter with Paul all day and ways to escape school. It was Friday afternoon, after all. By Friday afternoons, everyone at Melva High School acted like they'd been popping caffeine pills. Not the teachers — the teachers observed us with tired manatee faces, having long ago given up the day. The students, however, were buzzing, jazzed, humming with energy — the only time the Melva Hummingbird mascot made any real sense to me. The Hip-Hoppers had impromptu freestyle rap battles in the hallways during class changes. The Pretties and Beautiful Rich Girls switched to evening makeup after lunchtime. The Jocks and Jockettes gnashed their teeth and slapped one another more, ever battle-ready. Even the Bleakest Geeks shouted to one another their plans for weekend evenings of pizza and online gaming. Everyone spoke like his or her mouth had become a megaphone.

ANTHROPOLOGIST'S NOTE:

In the American high school, one must look his or her best on Friday. This is when all plans of any importance are finalized.

I met up with Margo in the hallway, and we picked our way through the stream of students to our final classes of the day.

"So, we're definitely going tonight, right?" Margo asked me, ducking out of the way of Nicole Petty, who was belting out a country power-ballad as she traipsed down the hall. I knew Margo was referring to Jimmy Denton's party. My heart quickened a little at the thought. Before I could respond, though, we were interrupted.

TR stood directly in front of us, blocking our path. She twirled a honey-colored strand of hair, blinking her large, teal blue eyes. She was a manga geek's fantasy brought to life.

"So are you going to Jimmy's party tonight?" she asked. Was I hallucinating, or was she smiling sweetly at Margo? Had her tone once again moved from Mocking to somewhere between Sassy and Charmingly Coy? It almost seemed like she was trying to be nice — like she was trying to win Margo over.

"Yeah, Janice and I were planning on it," Margo answered.

"Oh, cool!" TR brightened. "Well, I wanted to see if you needed a ride. There's room for one more with Tabitha and Casey and me."

Margo hesitated. I watched her jaw twitch. A frown flickered over TR's face.

"Oh, yeah," TR added. "And my older brother works at Michelangelo's. He said he'd totally hook us up with a fancy meal beforehand, maybe even a little wine! Girls' night out. I keep saying to Tabitha and Casey that I really want you to start hanging out with us."

Michelangelo's was the most pretentious and delicious restaurant in Melva. I figured that "Michelangelo's" was the only Italian name they could come up with since "Bella Roma" was already taken by a greasy pizza buffet. There were tiny, expensive, unpronounceable Italian dishes — a complete anomaly in Melva. And tiramisu for dessert. I loved tiramisu. I knew that Margo did too.

"Wow," Margo said, "that does sound good. Let me talk with Janice, though. See what our plans are. Maybe we could just meet y'all or something."

"Cool. Let me know." And with that, TR turned in a shimmer of golden hair and good clothes, slipping down the hallway.

Something in TR's voice — a pleading quality, a desperation to make Margo like her — made me wonder if she were not lonely too. A bitchy, beautiful, "popular" girl who occasionally needed to win a pretty new friend for her collection? Just to reassure herself that she could make people like her when she set her mind to it?

We picked up our pace, opening the side door leading out toward the vocational and arts buildings. I stole glances at

Margo's perfectly styled head. Was she seriously considering this invitation? Would she do that to me?

"Ha. As if you'd go with them! Ha!" I said, forcing hilarity in my voice. Margo just looked at me.

Maybe TR wasn't looking for reassurance. Maybe she was just a Friend Fadder. Like ducklings to bread crumbs, Friend Fadders were drawn to who- or whatever was momentarily attracting the most attention.

"Ha!" I said again. "Ha! Like you'd suddenly become all best-friendy with TR!"

Picking at a loose thread, Margo shook her head as if this were the most improbable idea in the world.

"Janice," she said, "you're my best friend. Just because TR is being nice all of a sudden . . ."

"I know, I know," I said, giving Margo a little half-hug squeeze.

"And maybe it's not that. Maybe TR's really, truly trying to be nice — I'll give her the benefit of the doubt. But I'm also not a moron."

"I know," I said again. "But really! As if you'd go with them! I mean, she's always bringing up your sister and the baby —"

"So? So what?" Margo interjected, her voice cold. "It's not like I'm ashamed. Let her bring it up all she wants."

"I know!" I said one more time. "That's not what I mean. . . . It's not embarrassing at all, I just think she means to —"

"Janice," Margo said. "I don't need you to protect me or anything."

Progress of a Friend Fad

Day 1: First Contact/The Wooing. "Hey, your _____
(attribute) always looks so _____ (positive
adjective). I've always thought you were really
_____(other positive and surprising
adjective)."

Days 2-3: The Wooing Continues: Wary Phase. You're now
sitting together at lunch, but you think it's a
fluke. Or you're suspicious. She probably only
wants to hang out with you because you're really
good at _____ (nerdy, academic strength).

Day 4: The Wooing Continues: Smitten Phase. You're
now in her thrall. It's mostly a subconscious
thing, but you've started mimicking the way she
_____(distinct and irritating habit).

Day 5: Showcasing. This is the phase where the Friend
Fadder flaunts your friendship for all the world to
see, perhaps by loudly hugging you in the hallways,
or by frequently posting private jokes on your
Facebook Wall: "Hey, remember that time we
_____(something inconsequential). Don't
forget _____ (nonsense phrase
vaguely suggestive of many hilarious things)!
LOL!!" At this point, you have matching
_____(type of cheap jewelry) from
Claire's boutique. You are convinced that your
net social worth has increased.

Day 8: The Slight Snub. Example: "Wow! Your _____
(attribute) is sure looking _____(negative
adjective) today. What's up with *that*?"

Day 9: The Blow Off. She's at a different table at
lunch. You think she might be laughing with her

other friends about you. Or else the fact that they're looking your way while they laugh is just a coincidence.

Day 10: Resumed Adulation: Example: "Girl, where have you BEEN? You are coming over Friday, aren't you? BTW, your _____(something you did) was _____(awesome adjective)!"

Day 11: Resumed Adulation, Part II: The Slighting. This bonds you further. She makes a nasty comment to you, perhaps about one of her friends she sat with at lunch without you the other day. "I can't stand Melanie, can you?! If you look really closely, you can TOTALLY see that she has all these_____ _____(disgusting physical attribute that is likely universal). It's *disgusting*! Let's not tell her about Friday, okay?"

Days 12–16: Repeat Cycle of Snub/Blow Off/Resumed Adulation. This, dear readers, is called "positive intermittent reinforcement," the most powerful sort of operant conditioning—just ask a gambler, or any girl who's ever remained fixated on a bad boyfriend who's mean, mean, mean, then suddenly and unexpectedly nice. It works. You will remain in her thrall. You will continue to _____ (distinct gesture you've picked up from Friend Fadder).

Day 17: The Drop. Suddenly, unexpectedly, she drops you cold. Maybe she doesn't show up when you were supposed to meet for a movie. Maybe she has an enormous slumber party and doesn't include you. Maybe she _____(something horrible and humiliating). You'll know when it happens.

We were silent for a minute. Then I forced a laugh, just to make things feel more normal.

"Oh, that reminds me. Has TR ever taken her shoes off around you?" I asked Margo. "Her feet smell just like the rotting possum we once found in our garage. Seriously — her feet are like two dead animals! I think she has a legitimate Stink Disorder or something. Maggot Feet. Ha!"

Margo looked at me again. I hoped it was because I was so hilarious.

"Wow, Janice," she said. "Wow. Please never point out my faults to me, will you? You're deadly."

I felt cold all of a sudden, my armpits gone clammy. The list Paul had made for me flashed in my mind, the word "hypercritical" bannering across my mental movie screen.

"It's just honesty, Margo," I said, my voice gone pleading and sharp. "Anthropology requires honest observation."

"Janice, you just compared TR's feet to a rotting animal. How's that advancing the cause of anthropology?"

"Yeah, but TR's said all sorts of stuff! Remember when she said you dressed like a schizophrenic homeless woman?"

"That's not the point," she said.

"I'm only being truthful," I said. "Someone has to speak the truth here in Melva, whether it's complimentary or not."

"There's truth," Margo said evenly. "And there's outright meanness. And someday you're going to have to figure out the difference."

Margo turned and walked away. I watched her go, my heart dissolving into liquid nitrogen in my chest.

Outside under the awning between the gym and main building, I spotted the two FreshLife leaders, Teri and Colin, the handsome guy we'd seen in the Mocha Cellar the other day. Margo waved and walked up to them. I watched through the glass door as they laughed and gestured. Teri looked like a future first-grade teacher: sweet, dumpy, and smiling, always wearing a sack-shaped skirt and Mickey Mouse T-shirt. She was filled with joy for the Lord, and harmless. She was the maiden aunt of Melva High. Colin, however, looked like he'd wandered away from a J.Crew photo shoot.

They laughed again, and I wished I could hear what was so funny. Being truthful in your observations is *not* the same as being mean, I told myself. Not exactly. So why would *someone* try to make you feel that way when all you're doing is honing your observational skills and practicing legitimate anthropology?

Someone walked up behind me and tapped my shoulder.

"Observing?" Jimmy asked me.

I turned to gaze at his scruffily handsome face.

"Do you think we should sugarcoat the truth, Jimmy?" I asked.

He shook his head. "Absolutely not. No way." He shuffled some change in his pockets for a moment. "And are you coming to the party tonight? You and Margo? I just want the truth. Don't sugarcoat your answer."

"Yeah," I said. "Definitely."

"Good," he said.

And momentarily I stopped worrying about Paul and Margo and focused wholly instead on the beautiful arc of Jimmy's perfect spine leaning against the wall. "Uh, yeah. I'm very much looking forward to it. It should be really nice," I said, hearing how off my words seemed. *I'm very much looking forward to it. It should be really nice.* I sounded like I was talking to one of the elderly ladies at church.

Jimmy nodded idly. "Mm-hm," he said. "Really nice. You don't go to parties, do you, Janice? Or not much, right?"

I wasn't sure how to respond. By "not much," what Jimmy meant was "not at all." He'd realized already that I was the Melva High Hermit. "I guess I'm a little picky," I said warily.

He stretched, straightening himself up, and then smiled lazily at me. "Yeah," he said. "I like that — I'm picky too. Anyway, I'm glad you're coming to the party."

With that, he walked away. I just stood there watching until long after he'd disappeared.

ANTHROPOLOGICAL
OBSERVATION #8:

Prior to approaching a male of higher social status in a public setting, the adolescent female prepares with extra care, decorating and perfuming herself for the occasion. She may even choose to do research.

At home that evening, I started to get myself ready for Jimmy's party. I opened my closet and flipped through my hangers. The sight of my clothes was dismaying. My closet was an Uglification Zone — and yet, determined, I searched, hoping to find something semicool.

MOVIE SCENE
JANICE WILLS: STORY OF A YOUNG
ANTHROPOLOGIST

The overlooked heroine readies herself for an encounter with her crush. One of those "getting it together" montages ensues, with some pumped-up girl music for a soundtrack, while she flings various garments onto the floor, applies makeup, and — ta da! — emerges more dazzling than ever before.

Of course, this did not happen. Nothing looked right. I felt stupid and ill constructed: Gangly McGangles all over again. Finally I settled on my coolest jeans and a drapey blue shirt that

I thought flattered me. I pinned back part of my hair the way I imagined a French woman would and put on mascara. I looked in the mirror to take in the effect: Gangly McGangles in her coolest jeans; Gangly McGangles wearing mascara. . . .

I still had a couple hours before the party, so I went to the computer to check my email. Nothing. I thought of Jimmy, how tonight might be my chance to talk to him. I had a mission: Mission Speak to Jimmy Denton at the Party Tonight. This required, as preparation, Operation Jimmy Denton Information Gathering.

So I Googled him. I typed in "Jimmy Denton, Melva, NC" and clicked SEARCH. I don't know why it hadn't occurred to me before. I waited, guilty, nervous at the computer, ready to close the browser window if my mom or brothers were to walk in.

But instead of merely finding name twins, I found the Jimmy Denton jackpot. There was his name a few times in the *Melva Daily Star* for placing in theatre competitions, and there was even a photo of him playing Stanley Kowalski in the Melva High production of *A Streetcar Named Desire*.

ANTHROPOLOGIST'S NOTE:
The Melva High production of the play had been edited due to parental concern over potential sexiness. Even though the changes had been slight, it seemed like a shame to me to alter the genius of Tennessee Williams. I especially respected any writer whose chosen name was a state.

The real Googling prize, though, was this: Jimmy Denton had a blog! The blogger profile matched him. His blog was called desperatemeasuresmelva.blogspot.com.

I sat reading it for the next hour and forty-five minutes.

I learned he liked tuna but hated mayonnaise, that he'd once peed his pants in the third grade and everyone had laughed at him, that he was struggling to pass calculus, that his dad had been stressed out at work recently, that his sister sometimes called him Boo Bear, which embarrassed him, that he had many thoughts on the various performances of Marlon Brando, and on Tennessee Williams, and on and on. . . . Part of one entry read:

> The play is absolute shit right now, and I told D. so to his face. But he's got a rock for a brain. Also talked to B. and we agreed to keep quiet about the whole thing. Now hating myself, this town, wishing I could escape. Later tonight, Dad heard that I failed the calculus test again on top of everything else that's happened recently, and of course he blew up. Flipping out and screaming at me, telling me he doesn't understand what's wrong with me, why I'm so messed up that I've got to mess up everything around me. My dad says I'm his biggest disappointment. He's probably right. . . .

I sat back from the computer, feeling another twinge of guilt. Although I didn't understand it all, the information seemed so private, so diary-like — and yet the blog had been easy enough to find. I couldn't decide whether to feel like a) a clever crush detective or b) an Internet creeper. So many of Jimmy's blog entries seemed angry.

The phone rang.

"Hello?"

"Janice?"

"Margo, I'm sorry about today at school. So dumb . . ."

"Listen, don't worry about it," Margo said. There was a pause. "I don't think I can come tonight. I'm just not feeling good."

"Margo! No! Please! I can't go without you!"

I could hear her silence on the other end, imagined the words collecting themselves in her mind before she spoke.

"Well," she said. "You'll either have to go without me or not go."

"But he invited us both!"

"Yeah, he did," she said. "But, Janice, I'm not going. I don't feel good. I don't feel like it. I can't go with you."

Her voice had the kind of icy solidity that made me not want to argue further. I wondered if she was still mad at me about the stinky feet comment.

"You really *can* go by yourself," Margo said, and there was a slight hitch in her voice, as if she felt sorry for me, or as if she were urging me to figure something bigger than a stupid party out. "Besides, it might be better that way."

"Fine," I said. "No worries. It's research for me anyway. I'll talk to you later, I guess."

"Yeah, later," Margo said. And we hung up.

• • •

I drove there in my mom's car. I couldn't remember the last time I'd done something without Margo. And I definitely couldn't remember the last time I'd been to a true party. Maybe middle school — a skating rink party. Parties, by the time I got to high school, had morphed into something I'd felt safer avoiding — too rowdy, too free-form, too terrifying. And yet I knew I had to go to this one. Never before had a chance to interact with Jimmy been so obviously presented to me. Never before had I been asked so specifically by my crush himself. I steeled myself with thoughts of the anthropologists I'd read about, packing up supplies for long voyages down snake-infested rivers in wobbly canoes. This voyage required similar bravery.

Jimmy's house was farther out in the county. In the darkness, I swooped down long, curving roads, passing cotton fields, barns, pastures, and every now and then, a house. I chanted facts to myself about Jimmy, our similarities — how we both liked *Hamlet* and old movies and couldn't wait to escape Melva, how he felt lonely too, all these clues gathered from his blog, as if they were a mantra — as if they would make us truly become soul mates.

When I reached his address, I saw only a long gravel driveway going down a hill, and all the way up it, parked cars, many recognizable from MHS. Seventy cars? More? I couldn't tell. I parked just off the road and started to make my way down.

I wasn't able to see the house from where I was in the tar-dark, but I could easily follow the sounds of voices. Gravel crunched underfoot. The low thumping bass of muffled hip-hop pounded toward me. The house, when I reached the bottom of the drive, appeared dark on the inside. It was a big, blank, parents-not-home house. I heard the sound of a fire crackling in the backyard.

I walked around back. A huge bonfire. Faces I recognized vaguely. Girls with long, bare, heavily lotioned legs sat on the laps of guys holding plastic cups. There was a cluster of people dancing. A keg. People milling everywhere, faces flickering in and out of the firelight. The rough laughter of guys kidding around, the coaxing yelps of girls.

I was here on the edge of the scene. I couldn't turn back now.

I thought of Ruth Benedict approaching the Pueblo people in New Mexico for the first time. I thought of Margaret Mead and the Dobu in New Guinea. I took a breath and prepared myself: Janice Wills, field anthropologist, about to enter the world of a true Melva High School bash.

ANTHROPOLOGICAL
OBSERVATION #9:

The traditional illicit beverage of adolescent gatherings is an effective cure to self-consciousness, but one must be careful of it.

I found myself walking, zombie-trancelike, over to where the plastic cups were being filled with warm beer. Dan Bleeker, the football player filling cups, was already wasted to the point of friendliness. He handed me a cup and smiled, sloshing my shirt a little.

FACT:
I had never so much as tasted an alcoholic beverage. Not even Margo knew this. Of course, I'd also, prior to this moment, never been to a true high school party. If some English class acquaintance ever asked me why I hadn't shown up to whatever big party, I'd try to play all this off like, *Oh, another party? Boooooooring!* and *Beer — disgusting! Over it!* It somehow seemed much less dorky to have tried something and decided you weren't into it rather than to be babyishly consequence-averse and good-girl-ish. Similarly, whenever sex came up, I tried to imply that it was old news — that I'd had sex so many times already that I was simply bored with it by now. Sex = Yawn Factory! Boredomsville! I believed in hiding my

hopeless innocence behind scorn whenever possible. (This, when I stopped to think about it, was essentially my life philosophy.)

I took the beer and sipped. *Ahh!* my Margaret Mead–self would have said to the native partygoer, *Your ritual beverage! Thank you, how marvelous!* But it was disgusting — I'd been right all along. Still, in the name of field research, I could endure this. I took another sip.

I thought about my personal mission, the one I'd researched: Mission Speak to Jimmy Denton at the Party Tonight. I'd just have to find him and then . . . tell him I liked his blog? Discuss Tennessee Williams? Call him Boo Bear? It was a plan in progress.

In the meantime, I had no one to talk to without Margo at my side. There were a few lawn chairs scattered about, so I found a seat from which to watch everybody, a darkened spot of lawn with a good view of the bonfire. Missy Wheeler was there. She'd found another one of the junior class officers, an At School Friend of sorts. They were talking intensely about some graduation-related matter. Missy, of course, had carefully strategized by bringing a little box of apple juice that she'd then furtively poured into a plastic cup to make it look like beer. I knew because she'd explained this strategy to me once. She brandished the cup like a secret pass, proudly showing it off. Watching Missy, I took another gulp from my cup. It was warm and gross, but I didn't mind the new tingly feeling coming over my body.

I watched Traci Oliver laugh nervously with some basketball

player. Seeing her butt cleavage showing, I wondered if this was intentional. Did guys find butt cracks peeking over low-rise jeans seductive? Becky Stevenson started running around, loud and giddy by the fire. There seemed to be this weird pride in showing off how drunk you were becoming, I noted.

"I'm sooooo tipsy!" Becky yelped on cue, and then collapsed into giggles against Trevor Jones. I watched them laugh and grab each other playfully, the undercurrent of adolescent hormones obvious. I took a sip. I took another, and another. Soon my cup was empty, and I was impressed with myself. I hadn't passed out, I hadn't gone crazy — I just felt peaceful and relaxed now. Since it was in the name of research, I figured I might as well get another cup.

This time the beer went down faster. I was used to it, the fermented taste, the not-quite-coldness of it. I was a highly skilled observer, the Jane Goodall of the teen species. I put my glasses back on to better observe. Missy had now found a small cluster of High Achievers who were still semicool enough to go to parties. She was laughing with them, forcing it. I could tell by the way they gestured that they were thinking, *This girl's trying too hard.* I felt sorry for Missy, but not as sorry as I felt for myself.

Soon I started to feel sleepily content, ready to chat with someone. I thought about walking over and inserting myself into Caroline Henderson's conversation, maybe say hi to Kip Stevens, but I didn't want to look desperate like Missy. Instead, I sat on my Jane Goodall chair, documenting the things I'd seen so far in my little notebook:

RESEARCH NOTES FOR *CURRENT ANTHROPOLOGY*

1. Four couples openly making out. The attractive one made it look really romantic, like in French cinema, but the other three couples, slobbery and ugly, made me want to turn into a robot so I'd never feel human emotion again.

2. Two breakups (both times, the girl was the one crying, mascara running thick and heavy down her blubbering face).

3. Two girls and one guy vomiting in the bushes where they thought no one could see.

4. One guy getting his pants pulled down by the older members of the soccer team. He looked like he was fighting tears before he punched one of them.

5. One joint.

6. Twenty-three cigarettes being smoked (at least it was good for the North Carolina economy?).

7. Five girls bursting into tears for indeterminate reasons before running into the house, flanked

by their girl posses. (Most of the girls seemed to move in clusters, like pack animals.)

8. One weird old man, definitely not in high school, yet who apparently crashes high school parties. He had a long, scraggly beard, sunglasses, and little suspender-shorts like Swiss hikers wear. Compared to him, I felt very normal, noncreepy, and age-appropriate.

I thought I saw Paul on the other side of the fire. So he'd decided to come after all. I thought of the list, the word "hypercritical." I thought he might have noticed me, even raising his hand a little as if to wave, but I looked away. And then I was startled by a familiar, deep voice behind me.

"Hey, Janice, you made it!"

I felt myself turning in slo-mo. My head was heavy, like I was underwater. In the dimness, I saw the dark eyes, the thick dark hair, the unreadable face.

"Jimmy," I said, "Jimmy Denton." My tongue was thicker and slower. It was like a furry rodent living in the hollow of my mouth, utterly disconnected from my own bodily control.

"Where's Margo? Wasn't she coming with you?"

"Sick," I meant to say, but it came out more like "thick," as if Margo were a really generous cut of steak.

"Thick? Oh, sick. She's not coming?"

I shook my head. I wished I'd worn all black and brought my

paperback copy of *A Streetcar Named Desire*. I wished I owned a push-up bra and took black-and-white photographs. I wished I were *cooler*. Still, I wanted Jimmy to sit down and talk to me. We would bond. He would prove to have a deep, artistic soul. He would fall in love with me. We would live in a loft in Brooklyn and have writer-friends and theatre-friends and anthropologist-friends —

Chip Hunter knocked into Jimmy in the midst of imitating some scene from an action movie for a bunch of guys by the bonfire. "Hey, sorry, man," he said, before backing away.

"Hey, Janice, so what's the anthropological term for 'asshole'?" Jimmy asked.

"Hmmm. I believe the anthropological term for asshole is 'Chip Hunter,'" I said.

Jimmy cackled appreciatively. I was hilarious. He thought I was hilarious! Something warm pooled inside of my lungs, filling up my entire chest. *Love*, I thought, *this is what love feels like*.

"What's the anthropological term for 'stupid bitch'?" Jimmy asked.

This jarred me. Maybe it was the term, maybe it was the way he said it — maybe it was the fact he hadn't immediately indicated anyone in particular. I gazed at him, unsure of myself. Slowly he lifted his arm and gestured toward Missy Wheeler. Missy was giggling hideously in a way that I guessed she thought was alluring. She kept touching the shoulder of some guy. I could feel her desperation even from a distance.

"Oh, the term we anthropologists use is 'Missy Wheeler,'" I

said, but there was a hard pit in my stomach as I said it. I looked at Jimmy again, gauging whether he was pleased. He smiled.

"You're great, Janice. Can I get you another beer?"

I nodded. My mouth was sticky-thirsty, like mayonnaise. Mayonnaise mouth. I remembered how much Jimmy hated mayonnaise, and my slow brain came up with a genius joke.

"Maybe something else," I said. "My mouth feels like mayonnaise. Ugh! Reminds me of bodily fluid."

He looked at me strangely. In addition to making a terrible nonjoke, my tipsy brain realized too late that it relied on information I'd read on Jimmy's blog. I wondered if this connection was immediately obvious.

"Not that anyone would ever drink mayonnaise. Or eat it," I said, my tongue still slow and uncooperative. *Shut up, Janice, shut up,* my mind hissed.

He studied me for a few seconds like he was Dian Fossey and I was one of the gorillas in the mist. I realized then that in the ideal Mission Jimmy Denton plan he would not associate my mouth with mayonnaise, but rather something he loved . . . like lime Popsicles, I remembered from the blog. Should I mention lime Popsicles? Was that too weird? Would that seem desperate? Was I desperate? Or was desperation the basic state of any mammal that has ever tried to attract a mate?

"Yeah, I'd love a drink," I elaborated. My voice sounded strange and tinny — like an old tape recording of me that had been played and played and was now warped. "I may not be able to endure the tribal rituals of all these assholes and stupid bitches otherwise. Please, bring me the beverage of the natives."

Jimmy laughed again and turned to head toward the keg. I watched him walk back toward the house. Maybe I'd scared him away, I thought. Maybe he was pretending to get a drink but really he'd just needed an excuse to escape me. Mayonnaise-mouth? God. What was I thinking?

Some other guys dumped more wood on the fire, and the blaze crackled. I smelled beer and smoke and a breeze off the lake. I coughed. Then Jimmy was back, holding two cups. He handed me one and sat down cross-legged on the grass beside me.

"So," he said, putting a hand on my knee. "I wanna hear more of your thoughts on Melva. Wait. It's too loud down here. Wanna come up to my room?"

ANTHROPOLOGICAL
OBSERVATION #10:

Intergender social transactions among the teen species are complex and potentially misleading. Thus one would perhaps be well-advised to avoid all opposite-gender interactions until one is at least thirty-nine years old.

I sat with Jimmy in his bedroom, looking at the posters on his walls (old movie stars: James Dean, Marlon Brando, Marilyn Monroe). I registered the details slowly, savoring them. My head was still murky with the three beers, and I wanted to close my eyes to rest, but I also didn't want to miss anything. The bedspread I sat on, the entire room in fact, smelled faintly of Jimmy. I inhaled slowly and quietly. I wanted to absorb every molecule of Jimmy-ness.

He had kept his hand on my arm as we'd walked inside from the party. He had talked to me. He had complained. *I hate these people. I hate this town. These assholes. What a joke.* In my swimmy brain, I'd thought, *How strange that even Jimmy Denton, seemingly the coolest guy in school, is just as miserable as the rest of us. How strange.*

He'd talked, and I'd nodded. Be quiet and throw in a few nods, and suddenly you become the most understanding person in the world. He told me, *Wow, Janice. I don't know why we haven't talked before. You're such an understanding person.* I'd nodded again. I *was* an understanding person — I was the Jane Goodall of teenaged behavior. I felt like I really *knew* Jimmy, down to his core.

Jimmy touched my arm again. *I feel like I can talk to you*, he said. Or did I imagine it? I was sleepy. I, Janice Goodall, nodded once more. I felt the sinews of his forearm, his curly arm hair. He smelled of Right Guard mixed with Head & Shoulders mixed with the faintest male sweat, and it was the most wonderful concoction I'd ever smelled. Every moment felt slowed, and I had the definite but not-quite-fully-formed wish that he would press down on top of me, the full weight of his chest against mine.

"Let's listen to some music," he said, getting up from the bed. He turned off the overhead light, clicking on a small lamp. He selected something melancholy, and I approved.

"I love this album," I said sleepily. "The Athens music scene has always been stronger than Chapel Hill's. I hate to admit it, but it's true."

He turned to look at me.

"Did I mention that?" he asked.

I couldn't remember. Had he? Or had I read it online? I couldn't remember now. Fervently, I nodded. Our conversation and his blog were blurred in my mind.

He moved back beside me and touched the wisps of hair on my neck, half-reclining, and my head roared like an ocean. I wondered if I looked prettier in the half-light, and sleepily adjusted my pose to soften the jut of my bony hip. Draping one elbow casually against my breast, I half-consciously tried to create the illusion of cleavage.

ANTHROPOLOGIST'S NOTE:
The female of the tribe offers courtship displays to the male.

"What's your story, Janice?" Jimmy asked, sounding meditative.

I shrugged. I felt like he wanted me to confide in him, but I wasn't sure how to answer. I was accomplishing more when I spoke less, it seemed, and plus, he was gently tracing one finger up and down my arm. *I want you to keep touching my arm. Please keep touching my arm*, I thought, and then, *I could help you pass calculus. Talk to me about how your dad is stressing you out — I want to be your confidante.* Instead, what I actually whispered was this:

"I dunno."

"There's gotta be more than that," he said. "We've got at least one thing in common. We both hate this place. This shitty town, full of shitty people, these assholes. Assholes who think they're the shit." He smirked a little at his own joke.

Listening to him, I wondered if we did have that in common. His tone was so angry, so hateful.

"I don't know," I said slowly. "I mean, I criticize this place a lot. I look around and I see things that I don't like. Things that annoy me."

Jimmy nodded, urging me to continue. I felt my slow thoughts crystallizing briefly into something that made sense.

"But, well, don't you think it's possible to be annoyed by something and love it at the same time — in a way? Maybe that's more accurate. Maybe I have more of a love-hate relationship with Melva. A fond annoyance, maybe?"

He looked hard at me. "That's not what it sounded like, reading your notes on the people at school. I didn't sense much love or fondness."

"Oh," I said. I tried to think for a minute before continuing. "I don't think I meant it that way — I didn't intend it that way, at least. Really I guess I'm sort of scared. Of a lot of things. It's easier to stand back and try to figure everybody else out. I'm not even trying to be mean. . . . But maybe it does come across that way. Now my friend Paul hates me, and my best friend, Margo, hates me too, and . . ."

I stopped, feeling tears gathering in my eyes. I blinked, collecting myself, wondering what had made me suddenly confess all of this to Jimmy — things about myself that I hadn't even previously put into words.

"Maybe it's really more discomfort," I continued rambling. "I mean, when I was reading your blog, sometimes it just seemed like you felt alone, and maybe that can sound like anger. So maybe you don't hate every —"

His finger had stopped tracing my arm, so I stopped midsentence. He frowned at me.

"You read my blog," he said.

I just looked at him as if I didn't speak English.

"What blog?" I asked dumbly. The beer made me want to close my eyes. This effort of articulating all these nebulous thoughts, of keeping them straight, was too exhausting.

"I have a blog, but it's set on private now. Or it's supposed to be. You need a password."

"Huh," I said desperately. "Maybe I did happen to see your blog one time, maybe when I was searching for something else," I added, hearing the terribleness of my own lie, the unbelievability, "but I can't remember exactly." I needed to change the subject. "Anyway — what's *your* story?"

"My story is I can't wait to get out. I hate it here." He paused. "My parents sent me away once. I was going to kill myself." He laughed a rough non-laugh. Cracking his knuckles, he turned away from me. "But you already know all that, right?"

I kept perfectly still, the way deer do when you drive by them at night. I definitely had not read anything like that on his blog, but there'd been a lot of entries I hadn't gotten to. . . . I felt a little dizzy.

"Mmmm-hmm," I muttered like a bad android, just to fill the silence.

He moved closer to me again and began gently tracing my arm again. I felt a shiver, the good kind of shiver, like I got sometimes when the hairdresser rubbed my head during the shampooing. With all of my Jedi mind, I willed his body closer to mine. *Closer, closer.* I realized that instead, I was inching my body closer to his. Maybe I hadn't creeped him out after all. . . .

"Your friend Margo is pretty, but I kinda like talking to you," he said as he moved his finger, tracing a line across my stomach — over my T-shirt, but still. I held my breath.

"You want me to kiss you," he said. Just like that. A fact. A mathematical truth. I closed my eyes to avoid looking at him. "I can tell you do. You haven't been kissed before. A girl like you."

The way he said it didn't sound mean — more like an observation. Objective. Anthropologically speaking, I could be categorized as a Previously Unkissed Almost-Seventeen-Year-Old Anthropologist. I felt myself float up to the ceiling, where I hovered, watching myself silent on the bed, watching Jimmy and his tracing hand — watching the whole thing.

That was when he placed a hand behind my neck and kissed me. *My first kiss*, I thought. *One of the ultimate rites of passage.* And it was happening here, now, with Jimmy. His mouth was warm and soft. My body shivered again and a low noise (mine) tumbled out.

I murmured, "I don't criticize everything. I don't hate everything. I don't hate you." Fortunately, my words were so low and garbled that he didn't seem to hear what I'd said.

Still holding my head, he said, "You know why I hate this town?"

I shook my head, every muscle in my body twitching in preparation for him to kiss me again. My whole torso seethed with warmth.

"I like . . . both. Guys and girls. It sounds stupid to say it. . . . My parents figured it out, and they want to send me away again. To this camp or something. Convert me back to normal."

I opened my eyes. He stared at me as his words settled in a way that told me I would never speak of this, never breathe a word. My mind had turned to mush, and I felt as if I were sinking into quicksand. He'd just kissed me. His words were confusing, but I still felt myself wanting him to do things that sounded like phrases from a romance novel: to *tumble against my body*, to *be the man of me*. All my thoughts were misfiring.

"I don't love anyone or anything here," he whispered.

And then he was kissing me again. This time harder. My muscles tightened at first in happiness, but then his tongue was pressing into my mouth, gross and eel-like. Our teeth were clacking together. He pressed against me harder, and it was crushing. It hurt. I gasped, but the weight of him was too much, and his mouth was hard and mean.

He bit me.

I pulled away, a tiny bead of blood oozing on my lower lip — and that was when I began to cry. Jimmy laughed a hard, mean laugh. His eyes were narrow and hard.

"Don't worry," he said coldly. "I'm not going to date rape you or anything." He laughed again, another hoarse, empty laugh. "Yeah, right."

He sprang off the bed. My eyes were spilling hot, fat tears. He turned his back to me and changed the music.

There was a knocking on the bedroom door.

ANTHROPOLOGICAL OBSERVATION #11:

A public weeping and gnashing of teeth represent the traditional ceremonial climax of the high school bash.

Jimmy opened the door. I was so jangled that for a moment I couldn't process anything. I took two deep breaths, and then my anthropological training kicked in — my observational skills, distancing me from the scene. I was merely an observer.

And it was Margo standing there. She looked beautiful.

ANTHROPOLOGIST'S NOTE:

A man in rural Zimbabwe often still must pay a *roora*, or bride price, typically ranging between five and ten cows, to the family of the woman he marries. The way she looked tonight, Margo would have gone for eleven cows at least.

From where she stood in the doorway, she couldn't see me. I sat crying silently.

"Hey," she said, leaning against the doorway and jutting out one hip. "Casey said you wanted to ask me something."

Jimmy looked at Margo, then back at me, and then back at her again. And Margo saw me.

"What are you doing here?" I asked her, sniffling. "You told me you were sick."

She hiccupped and turned her head away. "I felt, uhh, better," my former best friend responded, "so I went to dinner with TR and Casey and Tabitha. You'd already left, Janice. I called your house. And we hadn't really even planned to come by the party. It was a last-minute thing."

"You could have called my cell phone," I said.

Margo held up her hands in a gesture of exaggerated helplessness.

I wanted to throw up. First Jimmy had scorned me, and now my best friend had gone to dinner with all my sworn enemies? I couldn't decide if I was more disgusted by Margo's deceit, or by how impossibly clichéd it was — ditching me for a chance to hang out with the Beautiful Rich Girls. And then she happened to show up at Jimmy Denton's bedroom door?! In the history of classic teen betrayals, how utterly unoriginal.

I swallowed and said the following words to Margo very carefully:

"I hate you."

She looked at me for a few seconds.

"Whatever," she finally said.

Jimmy walked out of the room. Margo and I just stared at each other. My head was starting to hurt. I looked at the door and saw Margo wobble a little in her heels.

"Come on," she said. "Let's go."

Dumbly, I followed her back downstairs, back to the blurred

glow of loud voices near the bonfire. As we went by the keg, someone handed Margo another cup of beer, which she drank quickly. We passed faces I knew. A bunch of soccer guys chatting up two cheerleaders. Some Student Council Types and a few Softball Huskies ambling over for more drinks. A freshman in a pink skirt vomiting quietly by the bushes. Across the bonfire, Jimmy Denton hooked his arm possessively around some other nondescript girl in a skimpy dress. Everything flickered with firelight, the images drifting in and out of focus. It was unbearably sad.

Tripp Duffy, the captain of the MHS baseball team, sidled up to Margo and me, spitting dark tobacco juice on the ground between us.

"Ladies. You're lookin' lovely this evening."

Margo and I stared at him. Tripp was good-ol'-boy handsome, with a nose slightly crooked from a baseball that had hit him in the face, and the collar of his pink shirt popped.

"My buddies and I, we were talking. We said, isn't Margo lookin' good recently?"

Margo laughed, spurting beer out her mouth and nose, spilling some onto Tripp's shirt. Was she drunk? I wondered. Why would Margo be laughing at a compliment? Perhaps she had a case of contagious laughter, a psychogenic illness I'd once read about. She kept laughing, clutching her sides and guffawing at his great joke. Then I saw that she was also crying, tears streaming, and her face was contorted in a way that looked like pain rather than amusement. Even though I hated her now, I felt a pang of worry.

Tripp looked at Margo, looked at the beer spattered on his pink shirt, looked back at her, and sneered. "Dumb slut."

Coughing, Margo stopped laugh-crying and stared at him.

"Yeah, that's funny. Keep laughing. You gonna have a little brown baby soon too? Just like your big sister?"

And that was when Margo punched him. It wasn't exactly a good punch. Her arm was slow and uncoordinated, and her fist made only a dull, clumsy thump on contact, but the cartilage of his nose crunched slightly. And then there was blood.

"What?! Margo, what — ?" I said. Margo was still crying. I'd never seen her like this before.

TR and Tabitha ran up beside us. "What happ — Tripp! There's blood! Coming from your nose!" TR shrieked.

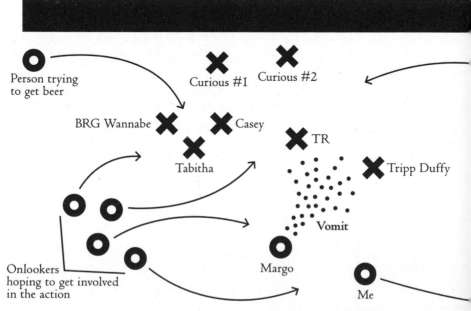

"Stupid bitch hit me. What's wrong with you?" he hissed, pointing right at Margo.

TR jerked Margo over to the side, her eyes flashing. She spoke in a low, barely contained growl. "Seriously, Margo. We liked you." She actually looked wounded.

Margo shook her head, doubling over. It looked like she might bear-hug TR or put her in a wrestler hold or —

Margo vomited onto TR's shoes. It was red and chunky and fermented-smelling. It made a loud splatter.

TR stared at her feet, appalled. Her lips twitched but emitted no sound.

I stared too, horrified, at TR's shoes for a moment before Margo sank to the ground. Sitting cross-legged, she held her head in her hands and began to sob and hiccup.

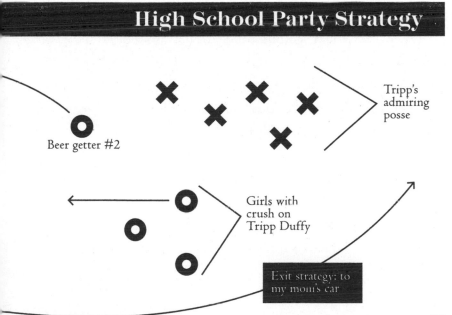

High School Party Strategy

Beer getter #2

Tripp's admiring posse

Girls with crush on Tripp Duffy

Exit strategy: to my mom's car

I stood before my supposed best friend, chewing my lip, the sour smell of wine vomit rising. Tripp and the others had scattered the moment Margo began to heave. Finally I guided the sobbing Margo back to the house through the basement door. We felt our way into the bathroom. I got a cup of water for Margo, who continued to whimper. Her face was runny with mascara and snot. She'd be lucky to get two cows for her *roora* now.

"You lied to me," I said from my darkened corner.

"Not exactly. Well, sort of," she whispered.

"How could you do that to me?" I asked, my voice breaking. "How could you choose TR over me? And what," I said more quietly, "were you doing knocking on Jimmy's door anyway? Jimmy — my crush, remember?"

Margo sighed. "Okay, first of all, Casey said he'd asked to talk to me. That's all. It was nothing. And second — honestly, Janice? I was annoyed with you. I didn't want to come with you to the party. You've gotten tough to be around. Your whole 'anthropology' thing . . . I'm sick of it. You're so negative. So tough on other people — so tough on yourself."

"Come on, Margo! Seriously? Anthropology is all I've got," I said. "That's not negativity. It's truthfulness. Accuracy."

"I'm not talking about anthropology. You've got to keep doing that. That's your thing," she said. "I'm talking about actually *trying* stuff sometimes. Not being all wry and detached. Not always commenting on people's weird habits or stinky breath and then comparing them to some tribe you've read about somewhere. You know?"

"No," I said, my voice rising. Margo's words had cut me like jagged pieces of glass, and now I wanted to cut her back. "I *don't* know. What I do know is that my observations of you are one hundred percent correct, Margo. You're the girl EVERYONE whispers about. You keep secrets from your SUPPOSED best friend. You flirt with guys even when you apparently also have some Secret Boyfriend. You think you're so pretty and cool and blah blah blah, but you're NOTHING. Nothing but a fake and a cliché."

"And YOU, Janice, are a fraud," Margo said, her breath hot and sour in my face. "You're afraid to do anything but sit on the sidelines and judge everyone. And you call yourself an 'anthropologist' like it's this great excuse." She laughed a dry, hard non-laugh. "Ha. You don't know the first thing about actual anthropology."

We stood statue-still for a beat, just staring at each other. I blinked back tears. Then Margo walked out of the house.

"I want to go home," I heard myself whimper.

FACT:
I sounded like a small baby mammal on a nature documentary, calling for its mother.

I stumbled back up the gravel drive to my mom's car, where I sat for a long time, crying, before I drove away.

ANTHROPOLOGICAL OBSERVATION #12:

. . . .

. . . .

"Janice, my sweet," my mom said, knocking on my bedroom door. "Are you okay?"

"Janice?"

"Janice?"

"Mmmmm," I answered through my pillow, holding my breath until my mom left.

I was thinking about my anthropology notes, neatly laid out, Word files and Word files. I'd always liked how my voice sounded authoritative and wise in those notes — in control, like those voice-over narrators on nature shows or during movie previews. I thought of Margo's angry words, of Paul's list, even what Jimmy had said about my observations. And it occurred to me: I was not part of the action. *Oh, God*, I thought. *I'm not an anthropologist. I'm the Lonely Voice-over Narrator of Adolescence. The Bitter Voice-over Voice.*

And the rest of the weekend was like this:

ANTHROPOLOGICAL
OBSERVATION #13:

*To understand a culture better, one must study avidly all means of
writing, art, and ritual, but one must not underestimate a key source
of wisdom: the matriarch.*

When I emerged from the blankness of the weekend that Sunday
night, I assessed. The postparty tally was: one pair of vomit-
stained shoes, one lost hoop earring from the pair I'd borrowed
from my mother, a pair of jeans that smelled of old wine vomit
and cheap beer, and zero friends. I would have to retire from
party appearances yet again.

I told my mom after dinner, "Margo hates me. Junior year
has turned into a disaster."

My mom replied, "Oh, darling. Y'all will make up! And the
Miss Livermush Pageant is coming up! Won't that be nice?!"

"Yeah," I answered through gritted teeth. "Something to look
forward to."

"Well, let's try on dresses for the big event, shall we? There was
a great sale at Belk so I picked up a couple for you to try," my mom
said. I could tell by her voice that she thought she was being help-
ful. She was almost as excited as when she dresses our dog, Pouncer,
in a holiday sweater. Almost. I took the first dress to try on.

ANTHROPOLOGIST'S NOTE:

If you are an American adolescent female and your mother picks out some on-sale dresses for you to try, they will never be beautiful. You will hate these dresses.

"Hold your shoulders back!" my mom barked. She tried to square my shoulders, making my shoulder blades stick out all the more. This dress was a hot pink concoction with a full, frothing skirt. It looked horrible. I noted with disgust the dark hairs sprouting on my bony ankles.

"Oh, don't you just look gorgeous! The bow really adds some nice volume to your chest."

The bow was very large and perched on my shoulder, covering my entire left breast. Correction: the area where my left breast should be. I had noticed that my breasts, or lack thereof, were actually even smaller than the breasts of Melva High's rumored-to-be-anorexic girl. Or else the Supposedly Anorexic Girl just had more naturally pointy nipples, giving the illusion of more breast than I'd ever possessed. This bow would hardly fool anyone.

"Honey," my mom called down the hallway to my dad's office. "Come see how gorgeous Janice is in this dress!"

I groaned. My dad walked in, studying me the way he studied the Dow Jones. His face was inscrutable.

"Looks great," he said noncommittally, but it sounded more like a hesitant question: "Looks? Great?" He paused a beat, and then turned back down the hallway.

"Pretty in pink to make the boys wink!" my mom yelped, clapping. "Well, let's try this other one too. They were both marked down!"

"I can't see why," I said.

ANTHROPOLOGIST'S NOTE:
Some cultures are less familiar than Americans with sarcasm. If I didn't know better, I would believe that my mother was from one such culture.

"Mom, you know there's really no point in doing this," I said, my voice breaking slightly. "I'll never win any scholarship money. It's hopeless. I'm a hideous wildebeest. I can't get anything right."

My mom cocked her head at me and gave me her squinty-forehead Wise Mother expression. "Sweetheart, I don't care about the scholarship money in this case. And you shouldn't either," she said. "Sometimes our victories are more personal. I just want you to *try*. And be brave. You're such a smart, thoughtful girl — I just want you to try something outside your comfort zone."

"You know I'm only doing all this out of anthropological interest," I said.

"Janice, you . . ." Mom paused. "I'm glad you have this special talent, this interest, but you realize it's not an excuse, right? It's not an excuse to avoid your own life."

My eyes grew hot, and I looked down. "Stop, stop, stop," I murmured to the floor. "Everyone keeps telling me this stuff."

"Janice? Janice. You're crying," my mom said. She lifted my chin so that I was forced to look at her. "What happened? Is it worse than I'd thought, what you said before about Margo and junior year being a disaster?"

I nodded, thinking of Jimmy's hard mouth on mine, of Margo's cold face, the words we'd said to each other, Paul's humiliating list. I cried harder and harder. My mom frowned, then pulled me close to her, stroking my head like I was a little girl again.

"Janice," she said. "Tell me, sweetheart."

And so I told her — a partial version of the story. How Jimmy Denton had seemed so artistic and cool, how he'd liked my anthropology research and invited me to the party. How Margo had been annoyed by me and thought I was too critical and liked TR better, but then showed up at the party anyway. How I'd gone for a quiet conversation with Jimmy that had turned mean — and how he'd basically told me I was an ugly girl no one would want to kiss and that he thought our main bond was that we both hated everything.

I looked up at my mom through my watery eyes. She frowned at me, almost as if she could tell she was getting only a partial sketch of the evening but that it was enough nonetheless.

"Janice," she said, her face calm and serious. "First of all, it sounds to me like Jimmy has his own problems to sort through — problems that have nothing to do with you. And as for Margo, I understand why you were hurt, but I have a feeling this is something you two are going to survive. What worries me here is how off your perspective is, how warped. Do you know what I mean?"

"All my observations are anthropologically valid," I said, shaking my head and burying my face in my hands again.

"No," my mom said. "Hear me out. I'm not such a bad observer myself — where do you think you got your talents anyway? First, Janice, you're smart as a whip. You're clever, quick — you're an interesting person in addition to being the daughter I love. Second, contrary to your own fixed belief, you're actually a pretty girl, not a hideous wildebeest. Third, you will not believe anything good I'm saying about you right now, not because I happen to be your mother, but because every teenaged girl is constitutionally incapable of fully appreciating her own good qualities. It's simply true of your species, your tribe. *This* is anthropologically valid: You cannot help the fact that you will not believe these good things I'm telling you."

I sniffed and looked at my mom.

"Sweetheart, you're wonderful. And I honestly think you've got a fighting chance to be Miss Livermush."

I scoffed, still sniffling. But I hugged my mom too.

"Well, be a good sport for me and try on one more of these dresses."

The second dress looked like something a mother of the bride might wear — a very elderly, very frumpy mother of the bride. Maybe even a grandmother of the bride. The dress was sea foam colored, with sleeves, and covered in long, dangly beading. I gritted my teeth and took it to my room to change.

"Mom, I look like a First Lady from the seventies," I said when I emerged.

"Nonsense! You look wonderful!"

"Not gonna work, Mom. Not acceptable."

"And you can move in that one too!" my mom said. "You can really get some good movement going if you need it. Like this."

She demonstrated, one arm going up, skipping from foot to foot. My mom was doing the Pony.

"Try it!" she huffed. "This will wow those judges."

Still wearing the sea foam gown, I threw up one arm and mimicked my mom, skipping from side to side. It was the most ridiculous dance I'd ever done.

"That's it! That's it! That's how a future Miss Livermush does the Pony!" my mom said. "Ohhhh, you would have been the queen of the dance floor! Chubby Checker would be proud!"

My arms were flying, and I was laughing, nearly gasping for breath. I collapsed into my mom, giggling.

"Thanks, Mom," I whispered.

She smiled at me.

"But I still think these dresses need to be returned," I said. "I'll find something else that's on sale."

Mom held up her hands. "Do what you like."

• • •

Later that evening I sat at my computer, frowning at the screen in front of me. Writing an essay extolling the virtues of livermush was the last thing I felt like doing. Partially due to Paul, the occasional vegan, I was a vegetarian — well, a fish-eating vegetarian, a pescatarian — and I hated livermush, a gross processed meat product. Still, I figured that stating this would not win me friends on the Melva's Miss Livermush scholarship committee. How did anyone write fifteen hundred words on a subject like livermush anyway?

I leaned forward, holding my temples in my hands. The glare from the computer screen made my eyes ache — made my whole head ache.

I thought about calling Margo. Maybe she'd been feeling lonely and wildebeest-like too — so much so that an invitation from TR and her crew might have been hard to turn down. I held the phone in my hand with her number there, ready to press SEND, but couldn't do it. I had tried calling Tanesha, my favorite friend from French class, thinking I might see if she wanted to hang out (although we hadn't ever hung out with each other outside of school except for when we'd worked on a project), but she had been out at the mall with friends. When I heard them all laughing over French fries in the food court, I chickened out, using French homework as an excuse. There, of course, was no French homework. *Girl, you lunchin'. You've been in outer space this whole week!* Tanesha had said, laughing. I'd desperately wished at that moment that I were eating fries with her, with someone, anyone. I'd even almost called my old junior cotillion dance partner, Petey Bivins, but then I remembered how I'd told the whole "date" story to Margo, how I'd laughed about Petey's distinct smell, all the while drawing (what I'd thought at the time were) witty anthropological comparisons. My eyes burned.

When my cell phone finally did ring, it was Paul again. He'd called a few times Saturday, but he hadn't left messages. I knew he was calling about the list. I knew he probably felt bad for upsetting me. But what could he possibly say anyway? I wondered. *Sorry for pointing out something that's obviously true?*

I almost checked desperatemeasuresmelva.blogspot.com but didn't.

There was only one thing to do now: type fifteen hundred words on livermush. I could take an anthropological approach. Heck — this could be a chapter in my larger piece on the whole Miss Livermush Pageant! I decided that this was going to be the best livermush essay anyone had ever read. The most anthropologically valid livermush essay anyone had ever read. And while I was at it, why not try a little? Operation Fighting Chance at Miss Livermush was about to begin. I was going to try this time. I began typing.

ANTHROPOLOGICAL OBSERVATION #14:

Unlike her predecessors, the twenty-first-century adolescent is less consistently adept at traditional performance work, such as dancing or singing.

Six days postparty, and I still had not talked to Margo. We were practicing the rigorous art of at-school avoidance. Aside from one tense run-in in the upstairs bathroom — Margo had refilled her bag so hastily to avoid me that she'd dropped her lip gloss onto the floor and left it — we hadn't seen each other. Walking the halls alone now, I felt like a woman in a space suit, invisible, apart, breathing a different atmosphere from everyone else. I missed talking to someone at my side. I missed having a best friend. I hadn't seen Jimmy once since the party. And I'd taken to eating lunch on the empty stadium bleachers, where neither Paul nor Margo would have thought to find me.

After finishing my Miss Livermush essay, I had composed a letter. It went like this:

```
Dear Wenner-Gren Foundation for Anthropological
Research, Inc.:

I am a great admirer of your publication, Current
Anthropology. I am writing to inquire whether you take
```

interns. I am eager and willing, and would like to get an early start in my advanced anthropological training. I would be happy to do this in lieu of my senior year of high school.

Please contact me if I could be of assistance as your intern. I would be willing to relocate from my hometown of Melva, NC, as soon as possible.

Sincerely,
Janice Wills, Anthropologist-in-training

I decided I'd give myself another week before I sent it. But in the meanwhile, I had to continue going to high school.

What I Did This Week
(Instead of Talking to Margo)

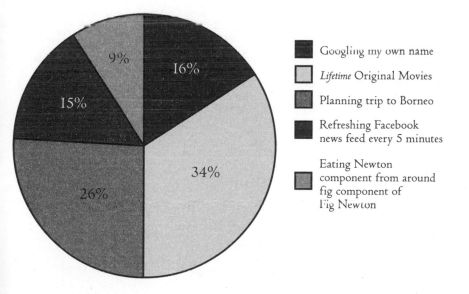

- Googling my own name
- *Lifetime* Original Movies
- Planning trip to Borneo
- Refreshing Facebook news feed every 5 minutes
- Eating Newton component from around fig component of Fig Newton

• • •

French was one of my favorite classes, mainly because it was small and Ms. Gerard was fun. We made French food and learned French cuss words. (Tanesha and I had gotten the idea to write one-act plays in French to practice our dialogue, and we'd argued that cuss words would authenticate our conversations.) Ms. Gerard had even done a whole lesson on French vocabulary words for cosmetics, since cosmetics are so emblematically French.

Tanesha and I were *meilleures amies*, at least for one full class period a day. I'd wondered if Tanesha might count as an actual *meilleure amie* — especially now that I'd ruined things with Margo. We talked a lot to each other, and I loved hanging out with her, but, still, she remained an At School Friend. She was a Cool Black Girl, and Margo and I were merely Socially Unremarkable White Girls, a subcaste of the Smart Pretties. The Cool Black Girls sat at a different lunch table, and they danced really cool-ly at school dances or on the sidelines of football games. In PE one time, Tanesha and her friends had tried to teach me to pop, lock, and drop it, but as I shook my scrawny butt to the ground, I worried that I looked ridiculous and pathetic rather than fun and willing to try new things.

ANTHROPOLOGIST'S NOTE:
The racial breakdown at Melva High was essentially half white and half black, with a tiny dash of "Other." People

got along for the most part, but mostly in accordance with the At School Friends system. At least we all went to the same prom, unlike some high schools I've heard about.

When Ms. Gerard turned to the board, I whispered to Tanesha, "Hey, Tanesha. Can you help me learn how to dance? In time for the Miss Livermush Pageant?"

She looked askance at me. "I thought you hated dancing."

"Well, it's Miss Livermush . . . and it's not like I'm going to get any points from the talent portion of the competition anyway, but I need to do *something*, and I thought maybe dancing wouldn't be too hard . . . if you could help me."

"You think I can dance because I'm a black girl?" she asked.

"Ummm. I think you can dance because I've *seen* you dance, and you can dance. But I'll be honest and say dancing was definitely not among the gifts handed down to me by my pasty Scotch-Irish forebears. . . ."

Tanesha winked at me. "Just leave it to me," she said. "After school today. Meet in the auxiliary room in the gym."

• • •

After school, I stepped into the auxiliary room and saw Tanesha and another girl. Their backs were turned to me as they both bent over a CD player in the corner. Tanesha looked up.

"Oh, hey!" she said. "There you are! We were just figuring

out a song. I'm guessing you want to avoid anything too hip-hop, but I was thinking maybe Beyoncé? Everyone likes Beyoncé, especially moms. All moms secretly love Beyoncé."

I stupidly had not considered what I would dance to. Beyoncé? Maybe this made sense. Something poppy, something crowd-pleasing, something in between Shania Twain and Shostakovich.

"Or what about Bob Dylan?" I asked.

"No. I hope you're kidding. Definitely not," Tanesha said.

"Okay. Beyoncé, then."

"You've got it," she said, "and hey, I haven't introduced you. Do you know Susannah? She goes to school in the county, but we dance at the same studio. I thought she might help. Susannah, Janice. Janice, Susannah."

The girl next to Tanesha stopped fiddling with the CD player and turned toward me. She smiled a friendly, radiant, beautiful Victorian girl smile. Her teeth were like a string of nice pearls. Her lips had a little cupid pout. She wore a tweed skirt and a ruffled shirt that would have looked dowdy on anyone else in the world, but only made her look interesting.

"Hi," I said, my stomach sinking down to my feet. "We do know each other. We've met. Through Paul."

Susannah, still beaming, walked over to me. As I was reaching out to shake her hand, she rushed forward to embrace me in a full hug.

"Of course," she said into my back, not releasing her embrace. "Of course! So good to see you."

"Good to see you too," I said into a mouthful of her hair. "Thank you for helping me."

ANTHROPOLOGIST'S NOTE:
People who have mastered the art of warm friendliness are far more annoying to hate because they reinforce the notion of your own hateful, bad personhood. All the while you are busy hating them, you are made sick with the knowledge that they probably do not possess a hateful bone in their body. Nor are you even worthy of their jealousy. It wouldn't occur to them.

Susannah gracefully pulled off her skirt and shirt, revealing leggings and a tank top underneath. She began stretching, pressing her hands all the way against the ground. Her body was like a piece of licorice. I was out of my depth.

Tanesha turned on the music.

"All right," she said. "Let's get down to business."

• • •

For those who have not had the experience of learning a choreographed dance: It is terrible. First, I watched Tanesha and The Friendly Victorian Beauty perform.

"It's easy!" Tanesha shouted. "We kept the routine pretty basic and short!"

FACT:

If this was basic and short, I did not want to see difficult and long.

They moved completely in rhythm with the song and each other. They shimmied their hips and did a little dip. There were a lot of sidesteps. *I can do sidesteps*, I thought. *It's just like walking, only sideways, rhythmically . . . and I can walk.*

Then I stood up and tried to follow along. I just let loose — gangled my gangles, lankied my lankies, shimmied my bony knees to the ground. It was not like Beyoncé's dance moves, but it was certainly as close to Beyoncé as I'd ever gotten.

But an hour later, I only had the first five sidesteps down pat. Beyond that, I got lost. I didn't fall on my face. I didn't trip. I just couldn't keep up. Everything was too fast, and my muscle memory was too slow, too feeble. My muscle memory was geriatric.

"You're doing great!" The Beautiful Excellent Victorian Dancer shouted. "You're doing awesome!"

It occurred to me how much more humiliated I would be doing this if she, Susannah, were also going to be dancing in the pageant. With Paul as her escort too. I swallowed, blinking back tears.

"Let's keep at it," I said. I was trying.

An hour later, we sat down and drank bottles of water. I still had not really mastered the routine.

"How am I looking?" I asked, a little short of breath.

"Much better!" The Victorian said with her sweet cupid lips.

I looked at her and wanted to cry.

"Ummm. Is there anything else you were thinking about doing for your talent?" Tanesha asked, grimacing a little as she said it. "Not that you're doing a bad job. Not at all. But it's new for you, that's all."

"No, no," I said. "I understand. Forget it. Hey, I made an effort, but I don't think dancing's my thing." I thought of the paper I'd written back in the fall, my genius paper "Margaret Mead, Melva, and Me: An Anthropologist Comes of Age in the Land of Livermush." That might work. "I'm an anthropologist. I should represent that to the judges. I could read this paper I wrote a little while back."

"Does that count as a talent?" Susannah the Lovely asked, blinking her sweet doe eyes.

"Well, *I* consider it a talent," I said. My voice sounded colder than I'd intended. "So it'll have to count."

"Are you entering the pageant, Tanesha?" The Victorian asked.

"No," Tanesha said. "I mean, I guess I could if I wanted to, but . . . I dunno. I'll be at the dance afterward, though. Everyone's going to the dance."

"Is it weird that way?" I asked. "This weird social divide? It makes me squeamish."

Tanesha threw up her hands. "Yeah, but I guess you could say I have other priorities," she said. "Livermush Princess is not high on my list."

I turned to Susannah. "What about you? Are you dancing as your talent?" I asked her.

Susannah wound a strand of hair around her finger and did not reply. Then she looked up at me. "I didn't have the GPA," she said. "I didn't qualify."

I stared at her. The GPA wasn't that hard to get, was it? It hadn't occurred to me —

"Hey, it's no big deal," Tanesha said, reaching over for Susannah's shoulder. "Who cares?!"

Susannah was crying! Just a little bit. She looked away and wiped her eyes quickly.

"I'm such a baby," she said. "No, it's not a big deal. I was just a little disappointed, that's all. School's not my thing." She looked at me. "You're really lucky, Janice," she said. "I mean, I'm a tiny bit jealous. Paul was always telling me how interesting you are, and you're smart, and . . ."

FACT:
My mind had officially been blown. Susannah, The Beautiful Victorian, with her retro aesthetic and her dancing ability and her status as The Official Girlfriend, was jealous of me?!

"Susannah, what are you talking about?" I said. "You're so beautiful and cool and talented! And being smart is totally different from being good in school. Look at Einstein! Seriously. I've been intimidated by how cool you are this whole time!"

She looked at me and burst out laughing. "Paul was right about you," Susannah said, smiling. "You *are* great."

"Thanks," I said, feeling generosity flood through me like June sunlight. I'd managed to help Susannah feel better, and for some reason I suddenly felt at least 24.3 percent cooler myself. She wasn't so bad, The Perfect Victorian. "We should hang out sometime — all of us, Paul, some others. Get a group together."

"Oh," Susannah said, blushing a little. "Well, sure. We're still friends, me and Paul. But you did know that we broke up, didn't you? A while ago."

I was so surprised I couldn't even say anything.

"Come on, y'all. I've gotta get out of here in a little bit," Tanesha interjected. "An anthropology essay sounds like the right thing for the Janice Wills I know, but let's practice this dance one more time just in case. You never know when you might need to impress somebody on the dance floor."

And we got up and did it. Or they did it, and I did most of it — and that was okay.

ANTHROPOLOGICAL OBSERVATION #15:

Common sayings and colloquialisms (e.g. those about time healing all wounds, the power of an apology, the glass being half full rather than half empty) seem to emerge in cultures because, well, they're all basically true.

I finally summoned the courage to call Margo the next afternoon and apologize.

"I'm really sorry, Margo," I said. "About everything. You were right about me. About how I was being so judgmental, such a jerk. I'm sorry."

"I'm sorry too, Janice," she said. "I still shouldn't have done what I did the night of the party. So stupid. Will you forgive me too?"

I waited a moment, silent, wanting badly to say yes but not wanting to seem overeager. Then, when I couldn't take it anymore:

"Of course! If you forgive me!" I blurted.

"Yes," she said. "Of course, yes!"

I smiled into the phone, relieved. It was like I could feel Margo smiling on the other end too, although all I heard was silence.

"About the Miss Livermush Pageant . . ." Margo eventually said. "My mom's driving me crazy."

I could imagine, of course, that facing Mrs. Werther would be infinitely worse than dealing with my own mom, particularly with regards to the Livermush Pageant. Margo's mom had not only won the MML Pageant when she'd entered back in the day, she'd won everything — every pageant and contest in western North Carolina. She'd been, and was still, beautiful.

FACT:

Mrs. Werther's greatest claim to fame was that she'd appeared frequently for some years in the first *SkyMall* catalogs — the one that's in the back of every airplane seat pocket — when they came out in the early '90s. Even now, they'd occasionally reprint photos of Margo's mom smiling while wearing a special traveler's neck pillow, or beaming at an orthopedically designed pair of walking shoes.

I'd also noticed that Margo's mom had a bad habit of occasionally violating the rules of the Unofficial Mom Handbook in the section on Raising Teenaged Girls — at least in the opinion of this anthropologist. Examples included: a) Giving a stern look and pinching the soft flesh at Margo's hip while she ate a second bowl of chocolate ice cream. b) Saying things like, "Horizontal stripes? Hmm. I don't know, Margo. Maybe someone like your friend Janice could get away with horizontal stripes. Not you, dear." Or c) "Asparagus! Oh, I just love asparagus! It's a natural diuretic, you know — I ate a lot of it during my *SkyMall* days.

Here, you might enjoy a little more asparagus instead of the dinner rolls, Margo!"

"She's upped her 'Don't eat that!' frequency," Margo told me now. "Of course, I still eat what I want, but it's getting to me."

"But Margo, you're beautiful!" I said, very much meaning it, proud to have such a gorgeous and independent-minded best friend.

"Why don't you come over?"

• • •

I hung up and headed over to Margo's. The whole thing made me so delirious with relief that I didn't even care that it was late on a Friday night. I knocked on the door, and Margo swept me into a hug. We went upstairs to her room. After a few giddy moments of chitchat, Margo turned serious.

"I'm so happy we're friends again," she said, sitting cross-legged on her bed.

I studied her, and then I swallowed.

"Can I tell you what happened? In Jimmy's bedroom the night of the party?" I asked.

Her brow furrowed. "Janice, no. Please don't tell me he . . ."

"No!" I said. "No! It's not like that at all. In fact, it's — well, it's sort of the opposite of that? Maybe? I think Jimmy sort of liked you, actually."

Margo nodded regretfully.

"And I think he's really angry. At the whole world."

She nodded again.

"Go on," she said. "What happened?"

I told Margo the story — almost every detail: reading Jimmy's blog, watching everyone, how Jimmy approached me, his bedroom, the kiss, the things he said to me. When I got to the biggest secrets, I looked down, fumbling with her bedspread.

"He's, ummm, he's tried to hurt himself before," I whispered. "Please don't tell, Margo. I feel bad for him. Even though he was really mean to me. I don't want to be the one spreading that around."

"What do you mean? Why?"

I shrugged. I wasn't sure if I should say any more.

"He's bi —" I started, then quickly, "like, 'bye-bye, Melva,' like, totally checked out. He can't wait to get out of this town and say good-bye because he hates it here."

Margo nodded. I wasn't sure if she'd understood what I'd almost said or not.

"Janice, that whole thing sounds horrible," Margo said, her eyes still studying me. "Jimmy acted horribly to you. But I have to say it's pretty cool how understanding you're being of him. All things considered."

"Well, I did delete my Jimmy Denton Facebook fan page," I said.

Margo smiled and hugged me.

I grinned. Something had told me it was not my job to out Jimmy now, not even in revenge. That would be up to him at some point. And somehow, by keeping his secret safe, I no longer felt so angry or humiliated by him. Like magic. For maybe the first time in my life, I actually *felt* pretty cool.

"If you wanna really be the number one best, Marg, you'll come with me to the mall and help me find a Miss Livermush dress. I still have to get a discount dress — Mom's orders. But I figure you're the best person to help me find something. Will you?"

She nodded.

● ● ●

At the Letherfordton County Mall the next day, everything looked brighter than normal. The Pick'n'Pay Shoes looked more fashionable, and the Chick-B-Quick's lemonade was a crisper, more neon yellow. Were people smiling more? For the first time in my life, I found the other shoppers to be, if not attractive, pleasant-faced.

"What's happening to me?" I whispered to Margo. "I like the Letherfordton County Mall today. Like, I'm *enjoying* being here. What's wrong with me?"

"Welcome to Club Optimism, young Janice. This is what ninety-five percent of the rest of the world is able to experience, at least periodically: a positive outlook. Greetings, new member."

We found the dress section of Belk. Berneatha, a store clerk in her sixties with bright orange hair and a quivering jowl, helped Margo and me.

"Darlin', we're gonna fix you up real good," Berneatha said, flipping through a rack of dresses as quickly as a Vegas card dealer palms cards, pausing now and then to pluck one from the rest. "Come on now. Let's show off those pretty arms."

Pretty arms, I thought, pulling the dress over my head. *Pretty arms.*

I looked in the mirror. The dress was a deep navy blue, and, well, the color flattered me. I didn't look terrible. Not a wildebeest at all. And the dress was on sale.

"Wow, Berneatha, thanks," I said. "The dress is perfect."

"Well, darlin', I'm good at what I do if you give me the chance," she said, bobbing her orange hair. Another day, I would have compared that orange hair to something hideous, like . . . I stopped myself.

Dear Mark Aldenderfer, PhD, I composed in my head. *What do you do when you realize that much of your research may be flawed? That you may not have been the cool, detached, professional anthropologist that you sought to be? That you were not quite approaching things the right way? Do you have to start over from scratch?*

ANTHROPOLOGICAL OBSERVATION #16:

The old-fashioned Southern lady has many specific ideas about the precise. way for younger girls to comport themselves, and these specifics must be imparted during lengthy and often embarrassing instructional sessions.

Thursday after school, one week to the Miss Livermush Pageant and counting. My personal checklist went as follows.

OPERATION FIGHTING CHANCE AT MISS LIVERMUSH

1. Fancy dress obtained. Best friendship rescued. Grateful shout-out to Berneatha in the Letherfordton County Mall.

2. Livermush essay complete and turned in: "Livermush: Food as Memory, a Proustian Reflection." (Best essay on the topic of livermush perhaps ever written, if I do say so myself.)

3. Talent chosen: "Margaret Mead, Melva, and Me . . . ," my best anthropology paper to date.

4. Search for escort abandoned. Escort = vestigial, antimodern. Not necessary to winning of Miss Livermush scholarship money anyway.

It was officially time now for the next ritual in the Livermush calendar. Mrs. Johnson, the civics teacher, held a meeting every year for all the junior girls who were participating in the Miss Livermush Pageant, so all of us knew exactly what this meant: Mrs. Johnson's Fancy Walking Lessons. We gathered, giggling, in the library after our last class period, waiting for Mrs. Johnson to appear.

I sat with Margo and Missy Wheeler. TR held court at a crowded table nearby, casting occasional glances in our direction. This reminded me of how relieved I was that Margo's and my friendship had been restored.

"You know that any girl who doesn't come to Mrs. Johnson's meeting gets kicked out of the pageant, right?" Margo whispered.

I frowned. "No way," I said. "This meeting isn't even officially required. They can't do that. It's just 'highly encouraged.'"

Margo scoffed. "That means required. Mrs. Johnson is big in Junior Charity League, and they always read applications. Bailey Williams got kicked out last year on some application formality. But everyone knows it's because she didn't come to this."

"Yeah," Missy added seriously. "And they say if you don't fancy walk your way to this meeting, Mrs. Johnson will blacklist you from getting a Debutante Ball invitation next year too."

She said this as if it were the equivalent of contracting some fatal illness.

I looked up as Mrs. Johnson entered the room. A hush fell. She was so old that she had student-taught some of our grandmothers. A former Miss Livermush, she'd supposedly once been a great beauty, one of the last Southern belles, but that was hard to believe now: She had a face like a dried-out string bean, narrow coat-hanger shoulders, and a bottom as big as two July watermelons bound together. She looked like a bobbling, raisin-eyed witch. But she knew how to walk — or had once known how. I couldn't see what was so appealing about her walk now, but no one dared question her. And no one ever mocked her — we were all too terrified.

"Young ladies," Mrs. Johnson began. "Welcome and congratulations. Y'all will be representing this high school at Melva's Miss Livermush Pageant. This is a huge honor and responsibility." She blinked her tiny black eyes and swiveled her licorice-thin neck, inspecting us. At least three girls, I noticed, were gnawing their fingernails.

"Y'all are LADIES. Southern LADIES," Mrs. Johnson bellowed. One of her watermelon buttocks jiggled as she stomped her dainty boot. "This means the following: no piercings other than earlobes — one per ear only, of course. No gaudy jewelry. No picking panties out of one's bottom. No scratching one's face. No sniffing and snorting. No chewing fingernails or picking lips."

I watched as several girls guiltily dropped their hands to their laps.

"No revealing pageant dresses. No gaseous bodily emissions."

A couple of girls giggled at this one. Margo turned to me, her eyes widened in amusement. Could Mrs. Johnson decree an end to farting, even in the short term? Declare all burps verboten?

I looked at her stony face and believed she absolutely could.

"Now, before we discuss walking, are there any questions?" Mrs. Johnson asked, her eyes again stalking the room.

We all looked down, refusing to look her directly in the face. Even TR gazed solemnly downward. No one raised her hand.

"Then let us walk," Mrs. Johnson declared. "A Southern lady walks with leisure, as if there is an invisible string holding her head erect — an invisible string to God above reminding her that she is His precious temple."

Mrs. Johnson demonstrated how a Southern lady stood, head high, black raisin eyes staring into the middle distance.

"She walks delicately, overstepping immodesty and mud puddles alike. She avoids the demonic wiggling of the harlot. She does not slink from side to side like a woman of loose morals but rather moves with the grace of a holy dancer."

I bit my cheek. I could tell all the girls in the room were likewise terrified and yet desperate to laugh.

Mrs. Johnson now began her full demonstration. Her head still unnaturally erect, she minced forward, her two watermelon butt cheeks quivering beneath the fabric of her prairie skirt. She did not look like a graceful dancer, but she did look like a woman who you wouldn't want to cross — a woman who could call her walk a Fancy Walk and then command you to mimic that walk without question.

"See, girls?" she asked, making a curtsy. "Now y'all will try it. Line up. Silently, please."

There was no question about this. No one dared whisper, much less crack a joke. We arranged ourselves quickly. I scrambled carefully to the middle of the line, figuring I might be noticed least here.

One by one the girls ahead of me began to walk. They stared forward. Some shook their bottoms a little. Others walked on the balls of their feet like marionettes. Mrs. Johnson yelled things at them like, "Head up!" and "Lose the hussy attitude!" and occasionally, "Brava, brava!"

Margo and Missy went just before me. They looked like awkward puppets, but Mrs. Johnson approved. "Good, good," she said.

It was my turn.

I kept my arms carefully at my sides, my head up. I stared at the middle bookcase on the wall and fancy walked like a ballerina. It was fine, it was great —

"You are a young woman, not a scarecrow!" Mrs. Johnson shouted. "Please! Act as if your limbs are not constructed of metal rods."

She was yelling at me, I comprehended. I was doing a bad job. I should join the Giraffe Squad. Stilts the Clown . . . I felt my face heat up. My limbs froze.

Her old talons were on my elbows, shaking them loose.

"Loosen up, loosen up," the old crone whispered in my ear. "Fancy walk *like a woman*, not like some grimy-pawed child who's afraid of getting into trouble."

My cheeks felt like they might combust. I stared into Mrs. Johnson's shriveled old face, her expression hard as a rock. And then, she winked at me.

"You could be the best one out there, girlie," Mrs. Johnson whispered again. "You've got the fancy walk in you. You've just got to step up and act like you believe it. If you don't believe it, no one else will." Then, speaking loudly so everyone could hear, she said, "Start over! Do it again! Not like a scarecrow this time!"

Shaking, I went back to the starting point, took a breath, and began to walk. This time I held my arms looser. I imagined a string holding my head up. I walked like one of those red carpet movie stars on E!.

"Better! Better!" Mrs. Johnson said. "There's hope for your generation yet!"

• • •

After Mrs. Johnson's meeting ended, I felt a mixture of relief and shame. I asked Margo if I should feel stupid.

"You weren't walking like a scarecrow the first time, Janice," she insisted. "Mrs. Johnson's fancy walking is what's stupid. She's so ancient that no one in the school wants to tell her this meeting is worthless. But you did do even better the second time."

"Still, I was the only one she made walk twice! Ughhhh." I groaned because that was all I could do — all any humiliated person is ever able to do. "Ughh."

"Besides," Margo added, "what does she know? You saw *her* walk, right? No one wants to look like that! This just makes her feel important."

I nodded. "Just another element to explore in my anthropology paper, right?" I said, smiling a smile weak as twice-steeped tea. "Part of adolescence in Melva."

I left Margo in the parking lot and went back inside the building to my locker. In all the excitement, I'd forgotten my notebook. I grabbed it and jotted down a few anthropological observations on the whole fancy walk experience for my research — Category: Pageant Preparation — before putting everything in my bag and heading back to the door. The hallways were quiet and smelled like pine-scented cleaning fluid. I turned the corner quickly, and as I did, almost bumped right into Paul.

He looked at me and opened his mouth, fishlike, as if to speak. But no words came out. I tried to screw my own mouth into a friendly smile, but something was wrong with it. It was too nervous, wrenched too tight and stiff to maneuver. So I offered Paul a weak grimace instead. A little pageant-queen wave.

"Hey, uh, hey," he stuttered. "What are you, uh, I mean, how are you doing?"

I nodded. "Good. Good. Just had Miss Livermush walking lessons with Mrs. Johnson," I explained.

He stared at me, his fish mouth globbing nervously again. I wondered then if maybe I made Paul nervous. Did I have the power to do that?

"I, uhh, I didn't expect to run into you," he said.

"Got-gotta run anyway," I stammered. "But great to see you!"

"Wait," he said. "Janice. Want to hang out for a little bit uptown? I can meet you outside once I run up to my locker."

"Um, sure," I said. "I'll have to tell Margo first because she was going to give me a ride. Meet you in the parking lot."

And I turned away from him and fancy walked down the hall. The real way this time. Even better than before. It was like I'd known how to do it all along. I was a natural-born fancy walker. If Mrs. Johnson had seen me, she would have applauded.

ANTHROPOLOGICAL
OBSERVATION #17:

The Palabadu people offer ritual garments made of butterfly wings to make amends, whereas the rest of us are simply able to offer a "sorry" or maybe an ice-cream cone.

Paul and I got into his car, and he drove us to uptown Melva. It was a sunny afternoon, and the neatly trimmed grass around the court square was a perfect, even green. The old buildings surrounding the square looked, well, I had to admit it: charming. We parked and got out.

"Wanna just wander around some?" Paul asked.

"Sure." I nodded. Ordinarily I would have pointed out that the verb "wander" implied one was in a place in which one was capable of aimlessness, of getting lost, of discovering something — a place completely unlike the short, straight, overly familiar lines of uptown Melva — but I didn't say that. With Paul, there *was* a feeling that we might actually be able to discover something strange and serendipitous through aimlessness, even there in that utterly familiar court square.

We happened to pass my neighbor, Mrs. Crandor, walking her poodle. Paul greeted her and she beamed at us. "Aren't y'all cute! And what a gorgeous day!" she chirped before toddling past us, following her little dog.

"Wow," I said to Paul. "Mrs. Crandor must really like you. She's never that nice."

"What are you talking about? She's *always* that nice. Haven't you ever talked to her?"

I thought about it for a minute. Had I ever talked to Mrs. Crandor? She was my nosy neighbor. I'd waved at her enough times — it seemed like I must've talked to her. . . .

"No," I admitted. "Weird. I guess I really haven't talked to her. I just thought because her face *looks* mean . . ."

Paul smiled. "Her face looks *old*, not mean. There's a difference."

I flushed. Paul probably thought I was hypercritical still. This whole outing was a terrible idea. I took a deep breath and focused on walking like a young woman, not a scarecrow.

"Hey," Paul said quickly. "Have you heard about the Palabadu people? In Micronesia?"

I frowned, racking my brain. Had I? The name sounded vaguely familiar. I'd read some articles about people in Micronesia, but I couldn't pull up the Palabadu.

"I don't know," I said. "Maybe. Are you finally interested in anthropology too?"

"Well, I was just flipping through an old *National Geographic*, and I happened on this article. The Palabadu have an elaborate ritual when they believe they've accidentally hurt or offended another person. They collect a series of special leaves — these large, waxy leaves that grow in the jungle. They use these leaves as plates. Then they prepare this huge feast for the person they've hurt. When the feast is ready, they summon the person and sit the person in a special throne made entirely out of conch shells."

"Maybe I've heard of this," I said. "Palabadu. It's sounding vaguely familiar."

"And the most treasured food of the Palabadu is ice cream. It's a luxury because very few people own freezers, and of course they live in a warm environment. So they prepare this huge goblet of treasured ice cream with caramel sauce for the person they feel they've wronged, and they also offer her a handmade ceremonial garment made entirely of butterfly wings —"

"You're kidding me," I said. "No freezers but they love ice cream? Butterfly wings? What issue was this?"

Paul grinned at me. He shrugged.

"Seriously, Paul? Where'd you hear this stuff?"

"Fine," he said. "You figured me out. I made it all up. No Palabadu. But it sure sounds like a nice culture, right? And what I'm trying to tell you is . . . I think I owe you ice cream."

I smacked his arm lightly. "You liar! And of course here I am telling you that the Palabadu sound familiar." I laughed, shaking my head.

So Paul and I walked down the street and around the corner to the Melva Ice-Cream Shop. The ice-cream shop was a popular afternoon spot mostly for middle schoolers, but sometimes when we got the urge for ice cream, we still went there too. The door jingled as we walked inside.

"Hey, buddy!" Paul called.

Stephen Shepherd was sitting at one of the tables. He put aside a jumble of tiny objects in front of him and looked up happily. His face was muddy with chocolate ice cream.

"Hey, Paul!" Stephen said. He looked at me warily, then back at Paul.

"Looks like you got into a serious battle with that ice cream, but still managed to triumph," Paul said, laughing. "What have you got there?"

Stephen looked at the jumble in front of him. Tiny gears and cogs and silvery whatnots.

"Model plane parts. Miniature," he said. "Started working on this sort of thing at MIT this past summer. But I'm building my own design and hoping eventually to translate it to the real deal."

What was it that was so weird about Stephen? I wondered. And then I realized — he looked perfectly happy. Perfectly happy doing exactly what he liked, even if he looked like a chocolate-covered three-year-old playing with Legos.

ANTHROPOLOGIST'S NOTE:
The sight of an adolescent looking utterly happy is so unusual that it is startling.

"That's cool, Stephen," I said. "I had no idea you were so good."

He smiled back at me. A brown-toothed, sticky-faced smile, but a good smile nonetheless.

Paul and I ordered ice cream, and when he was about to pay, Mr. Thompson, the shop owner, stopped him. "Wait. Wait. If I'm not mistaken, you're buying ice cream for one of our Miss Livermush contenders. Is that correct?" he asked, winking at me.

"Uh, yes. Yes, sir," I said. "I'll be there next Saturday. Gonna give it my best shot."

"Well, that's all anyone can ask, isn't it? Ice cream's on the house for both of you. Good luck Saturday!" Mr. Thompson said.

"Wow," I said as we walked outside to find the benches. "That was so nice of Mr. Thompson. And I didn't realize Stephen was so smart."

"Yeah," Paul said. "He's pretty brilliant — especially when it comes to mechanical stuff. Aviation. That sort of thing."

I nodded, licking the side of my ice cream before it could drip. "Yeah, I guess I always only noticed how weird he was."

Paul grinned at me. "Everybody who's really into something is weird. You too. What's the weirdest thing you've done in the name of anthropology?"

I thought for a minute. "I used to go to this online anthropology chat room. It was mainly for grad students and professors," I said. I told Paul a little about it. The discussions were often mundane but occasionally interesting, especially when someone wrote about his fieldwork. At the time, I'd gathered that most of the people I talked to were also eccentrics — odd, bald, lonely but harmless men in Hot Pocket–stained clothes — but I convinced myself that the more unglamorous the person with whom I was engaged in anthropological conversation (online, at least), the greater the intrinsic intellectual merit. Possibly. Of course, I'd been hoping there might be a devastatingly handsome young anthropologist among them too.

"But then one day AnthropoManiac75 from Indiana told me that we were soul mates and he'd already Googled me and found my family's address, so I've avoided the anthropology chat room ever since," I said.

Paul guffawed. "Seriously?! And had AnthropoManiac found your address?"

"No, of course not! He was lying. He didn't even know my real name. I'm not stupid! But probably best not to mention it to my mom," I said. "She's watched one too many television news shows on Internet predators." This was true: My mom seriously viewed the Internet as nothing more than one big child molester hangout buzzing with constant ENLARGE YR PENIS emails and pornography.

I watched Paul slurp his ice cream — there was something cute about it. I looked at his mouth, thinking briefly of Jimmy's mouth hard against mine. I couldn't imagine Paul's mouth doing or saying anything unkind.

"What's the weirdest thing you've done?" I asked Paul.

"My entire life," he said. "My entire life is composed of weird things I've done in the name of some interest or another."

"And so you struggle to downplay all the weird things you do in order to survive, huh?" I said. "Get by without attracting too much notice?"

Paul tilted his head at me, studying my face. Slowly he began to shake his head.

"No, no, no, Janice," he said. "I thought you were a better anthropologist than that! You have the entire art of adolescent survival all wrong! You don't *hide* your weirdnesses. You embrace them, thereby making them *cool*. It becomes your whole appeal, your strategy. And it works every time. It's basically punk. A punk rock approach to life."

I looked at Paul for a second before I burst out laughing again. "I hate to break it to you, but you're soooooo not punk," I said, still laughing. "You may have figured some things out, but you're no Joey Ramone."

Paul shrugged again, smiling.

"It's like making it to the next video game level when you think you've already conquered the game, Janice," he continued. "You've heard of the pink of goth, right? Like, if you're so goth that the goth-est thing you can do is to ditch the safety pins and rock something pastel pink instead? That's like me being punk. That's how punk I am — I'm so punk, I'm the easy listening of punk. I'm totally the Lite FM of punk rock. It's a full-circle thing, you see?"

"I hear you," I said, smiling. "And I'm like, the pleated khaki high-waters of cool. The thick lenses and headgear of hip. So utterly, transcendentally cool that the next level upward is basically polka-dot suspenders. It's a nerd of cool situation."

Paul laughed. I watched him, his crinkling brown eyes, his straight teeth, his wavy brown hair. *Cute*, the non-anthropologist part of my brain warbled inside my head. *Very cute.*

My cell phone rang.

"Crap," I said. "It's my mom. I've got to go, but Paul, thank you for the ice cream. And for sharing the wisdom of the Palabadu."

"No problem," he said, "and good luck in the pageant. Own it. Nerd of cool, represent. I'll see you there."

ANTHROPOLOGICAL OBSERVATION #18:

A pageant provides a codified public situation during which one may gaze, assess, and judge the relative merits of individuals without facing reprimand for doing so.

It was finally Saturday morning, the day of the annual Melva's Miss Livermush Pageant and Scholarship Competition. I felt like I'd been guzzling energy drinks. I hadn't, of course — I hadn't been able to eat or drink anything but water because I was so nervous. My dress was wrapped carefully in plastic. Margo and I walked past the booths and food stands already set up for the Livermush Festival to the registration table.

Standing in line, my arms goose-bumped. Margo shivered beside me.

"I hope it warms up," I said to the lady at the registration table, looking up at the grayish sky, "and doesn't start pouring."

HISTORICAL NOTE:
Once, at the Melva's Miss Livermush Pageant of 1953, it started pouring. With thunder and lightning. A tree near the stage was struck by lightning and two contestants were injured — only mildly. Still, a rule was

instituted that the pageant be called off at the first sound of thunder.

"Trust me, you'll be so nervous you won't notice anything up there," the registration lady said reassuringly. "It'll be like this weird dream that'll be over before you know what happened."

"Okay," I said, smiling at her like a mechanical doll.

As we walked away, Margo whispered to me, "That was the least encouraging bit of encouragement I've ever heard."

Margo and I followed the pageant coordinator, Ms. Anne Whitaker, to the greenroom that had been set up in the Arts Council building. All the girls were assigned a chair and a small cubby by the mirrors. We would change and get ready there. Ms. Whitaker explained all this quickly without blinking. She was a news anchor on the local channel's *Melva Headline News*, a position that hardly seemed like a real job to me but apparently required monstrous amounts of pancake makeup even when not in front of television lights.

The pageant's theme this year was "Tropical Wonderland!" so there were huge papier-mâché flowers, birds, and butterflies everywhere — on the stage, backstage, and in the greenroom as well. I had to admit that the enormous, multicolored flowers were impressive.

"Who did the decorations?" I asked Ms. Whitaker.

"Oh, a nice young man from Melva High School that we hired — quite a versatile artist. Jimmy Denton? Do you girls know him? We explained our vision to him, and he gave us this. We couldn't have been more pleased with the result!"

I faced the floor, my cheeks burning.

"All right, girls. Here you go. Blair here is helping us. She'll direct you and make sure you're ready for the stage at the appropriate times. She can answer any questions because she went through this experience last year."

Blair happened to be TR's older sister, a former Miss Livermush herself. She had dark, silky hair and large, long-lashed eyes. She looked at us with zero expression.

"There," she said, indicating a dressing space with a limp finger. "Go to it." And then she yawned. Clearly Blair had better things to be doing.

Then, "Heeeey, lady, you look GORGEOUS!" Blair's voice boomed, all of a sudden becoming Little Miss Enthusiasm. "Wow, who did your makeup? You're gonna look so good up there!"

It was Theresa Rose. She DID look gorgeous. She was already wearing a sleek black dress. Her long blond hair was piled on her head, and she had on dangly earrings so perfect that I could feel the toddler-urge to grab them from her ears and make them mine. TR saw us looking at her, and waved before turning to her bag to get ready. The clean lines of her back and shoulders shone golden.

I was not jealous for the following reasons:

I. Jealousy is an unbecoming emotion, and so I refused to experience it, and besides,

2. black formal dresses (*so the default option! boring!*) demonstrated a complete lack of creativity, whereas navy blue — well, now that's adventure!

3. Jane Goodall, with her great, generous intellect, would never have been jealous of something so superficial and petty.

I turned to my own cubby to get ready. Missy Wheeler, her auburn hair now perfectly offset by the purple bodice of her dress, was using the cubby between Margo's and mine. She was deeply immersed in mascara application beside me. She had a special technique that involved separating each lash with a safety pin. I, on the other hand, was a fluster of powders and lipstick. It had all looked perfect in the packaging, but somehow when I applied makeup, it never seemed to beautify as much as I hoped.

Missy frowned at herself in the mirror.

"Come on, Janice," she said. "Wanna step outside and check our makeup? You can tell better in the natural light."

She grabbed a small mirror, and I followed her outside.

"Hey."

Missy and I turned. Jimmy Denton stood behind us in worn jeans and a T-shirt. He held a few papier-mâché flowers and birds in his arms.

"Hey, good luck, y'all. Good luck, Janice."

He seemed nervous, almost apologetic. My tongue froze.

"Janice, uhh, I just wanted, uhh . . ."

He kicked a piece of string on the ground and trailed off. Total Awkwardness Olympics. Missy interrupted with her Teacher Voice.

"Thanks soooo much, Jimmy. Your decorations are amazing. Really cool. Janice was admiring them."

He nodded and walked away. I looked at her, horrified.

"Did not," I said to Missy. Using the tiny compact mirror, I started to apply the mascara I'd borrowed from my mom. I hoped to look doe-eyed like Susannah or like Audrey Hepburn or even mean, pretty-eyed Blair. My hands were still shaking, though.

"Did not what?" Missy asked.

"I did not admire his decorations. I can't stand that guy."

"Janice, here. Let me help you with that. I think your mascara might be, like, a hundred years old. Let's use mine."

I sighed and dropped the crusty mascara, then faced Missy, holding carefully still. She was good at makeup when it was called for, precise in her application. It soothed me to have someone touch my face gently. Missy studied my face in the sunlight, clicked her tongue approvingly, and then we headed back inside.

As soon as we returned, Blair appeared behind us again, her pretty face once more blank and cold.

"Don't be disappointed if you don't win," she purred. "Not everyone's really made for the pageant scene, and it's the trying that counts." She smiled wickedly. "Besides, the world needs women who can work in labs and offices without being a distraction." She winked at us and walked away.

Missy's face was blazing, and she fumbled with the makeup brushes. Strangely, Blair didn't bother me at all. *Nerd of cool*, I thought. Blair, it occurred to me, was devastatingly boring. I felt bad for her.

But Blair had messed with Missy's head all right. I spent the next fifteen minutes whispering reassurances to her. "Blair's just a Sour Face," I said. "Don't worry about her — I mean, she's TR's *sister*," and "You'll never end up in some boring office. You're VERY distracting."

ANTHROPOLOGIST'S NOTE:
def. *Sour Face*: (n) a girl who always looks as if she's experiencing a distinctly unpleasant bitter taste and maintains this dour facial expression regardless of what her actual emotions are. Such a girl is impossible to read.

There was no time to dwell on Blair's baditude, though. It was time for the Miss Livermush Pageant to begin.

ANTHROPOLOGICAL OBSERVATION #19:

Performance and public shaming are often virtually identical experiences, differentiated only by context. And often even then, not that different.

ANTHROPOLOGIST'S NOTE:

The Melva's Miss Livermush Pageant and Festival began in 1924. According to local lore, sixteen-year-old Charalena Blanton, the daughter of a prominent local cotton grower, told her beloved papa that there should be a festival in Melva, and that she would like to be the queen of said festival. After much chin-scratching, Mr. Blanton suggested that perhaps a Cotton Queen or Cotton Festival might please his daughter (as this was, after all, the basis of the local economy), but young Charalena instead declared that she would like for the festival to celebrate her favorite local foodstuff, livermush. And thus the Livermush Festival and Miss Livermush began. The festival became an annual event (except for about a five-year hiatus during the Great Depression), and yes, you guessed it: Charalena was the first winner of the pageant, the very first Melva's Miss Livermush.

ADDITIONAL NOTE:

It's also said that Charalena was not terrifically beautiful. In fact, it seems she was missing a great many of her teeth. At that point, academics were not taken into consideration either. But Papa Blanton happened to be footing the festival bill for those first couple years, so that probably outweighed any concern over dental pulchritude and helped the judges make their decision.

Among my twenty-first-century Miss Livermush competitors, however, it seemed that a full set of teeth was now de rigueur. The stage for our competition was set up outdoors, facing the historic courthouse (now a Civil War museum). Metal folding chairs had been set up in rows for what looked like miles.

Maybe it would storm, I thought. *Maybe there'd be a tornado. Maybe the world would end* — but not fast enough. Already the pageant had started.

I found Margo in the wings and wedged myself next to her among all the other sixteen- and seventeen-year-old girls in tight, stiff dresses. Quarter-sized drops of cold sweat rolled down my armpits. We were a squirming mass of fabric, struggling to get a view out to the audience. I blinked, sans glasses, and saw only a swirl of blank putty faces and shirt colors.

Ms. Whitaker made welcomes and introductions into the microphone. The delay in the sound system made it nearly impossible to hear what she was saying from backstage, but periodically she paused for bursts of audience applause. Then Blair was pushing us out onstage, hissing, "Go, go! Now!"

I clomped along, following the herd of girls. "You Are So Beautiful" blared out over the speakers. We crammed onto the stage. Some girls waved cheerily to a parent or sibling in the crowd. Blind without my glasses, stunned, I focused on staying as far in the back as possible.

Ms. Whitaker stood in the front and explained to the crowd, "We want to congratulate all of these young ladies onstage. They are all outstanding juniors at their respective high schools. They all represent Melva livermush — but only ONE young lady will be crowned this year's Melva's Miss Livermush! Now, the judges have already narrowed the contestant pool to a group of finalists based on GPA, teacher recommendations, and an essay. These twenty young ladies will continue in the talent and interview portion of the Miss Livermush contest!"

The crowd roared in enthusiasm. Was there really nothing better for these people to do on a Saturday morning than watch a bunch of dorky-looking girls in dresses on a stage? I groaned silently, hoping to make it through the pageant as early and as unembarrassingly as possible.

Contest helper-ladies in corsages were patting the chosen finalists on the shoulder and beckoning them to the front of the stage. Each chosen girl invariably squealed and clasped her hands. Mostly they were girls I didn't know, from the county high school, but then Margo was selected. She smiled and moved forward. And then, with the loudest squeal yet, Missy. In the final moment, I too felt my shoulder touched. The unselected girls cleared the stage, and I saw that TR, Casey, Tabitha, and some of TR's cheerleading minions were in the final twenty as well. Camera flashes went off. The audience members clapped and shouted. Sweating, I tried to force a movie star smile. The mascara on my lashes felt like glue. I thought I heard my mom hooting, loud and happy, her voice rising above the other female voices in the crowd.

When the applause died down, Ms. Whitaker and Blair huddled the twenty finalists together in the wings.

"All right, girls. As you were told, you are to be prepared at this point to perform your talent. We'll have a fifteen-minute break while the dancers from Miss Debbie's Broadway Star Dance Academy perform a couple numbers, and then it's back onstage in the randomly assigned order listed. That means first we have Grace Alton. I'll post the list here in the wings. Go get ready!"

We scampered, tripping over our dresses, back to the green room.

"Oh, God, oh, God, oh, God," Missy mumbled next to me. I knew that Missy, after wracking her brain for some performable talent, had decided to rediscover her third-grade tap-dancing skills.

In the dressing area, I sat numbly watching the flurry of changing and nervous chatter. I pulled out my notebook and observed them, noting how each girl handled her nervousness, eyeing each tic and superstitious ritual. Girls who hadn't progressed in the contest came up to friends and hugged them, wishing them luck, until Blair shooed them away. I didn't need to change clothes for my talent, but Missy was shimmying her way into a spangled tap costume with tiny fringe skirt and tights.

"Oh, God, oh, God, oh, God," she repeated.

"You'll be great, Missy. You're a star," I said.

She furrowed her brow, adjusting the crotch of her costume. "You're still reading an essay as your talent performance? Not the livermush essay, though, right? The anthropology one?"

I nodded. The others would razzle-dazzle in sparkly clothes, whereas I would finally showcase some of my anthropological fieldwork. Maybe it wasn't what people traditionally considered a performable talent, but I'd worked hard on my anthropology paper. It was full of what I hoped would be stunning and incisive observations.

• • •

After the dancers finished, we finalists stood backstage, waiting, sweating, as Grace Alton began. She did ballet to a Johnny Cash song. The subsequent early acts seemed to happen amazingly fast. A couple girls sang. There was a flute, a violin, and, of course, three piano pieces. Three dances: two ballet, one modern.

Breakdown of Talents Performed at Melva's Miss Livermush Pageant

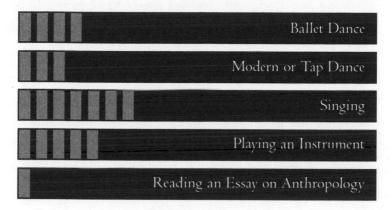

Ballet Dance

Modern or Tap Dance

Singing

Playing an Instrument

Reading an Essay on Anthropology

ANTHROPOLOGIST'S NOTE:

The term "talent" is strange and elusive and open to interpretation. It is said that Charalena Blanton, the first Miss Livermush, performed cornhusk dolls as her talent. By this I mean that she got up onstage with cornhusks and made dolls while the admiring crowd watched. Part of me has to really respect this girl.

I peered out from the curtains, watching each act. All of us hovered, silently rating our competitors.

"Our next performer, from Melva High School, is Missy Wheeler! She'll be tap-dancing to 'There's No Business Like Show Business.'"

The music started. Waving and beaming like Shirley Temple, Missy tapped out onstage. The crowd cheered.

Watching her, I felt embarrassed for Missy but not humiliated. She moved simply and clumsily — *tap tap tap*. Nothing fancy, kind of childish. She looked exactly like what she was: a girl who'd learned some rudimentary tapping in third grade, and now had thrown together a last-minute tap routine years later. But she didn't fall down, no one booed, and she finished the number. I flushed with desperate jealousy. It was a generous crowd, and once again, they cheered wildly when the song finished.

In the wings again, a flushed, sweating Missy swooped toward me for a hug.

"I did it!" she whispered.

"You were great!" I said.

Five more girls went onstage, faster and faster it seemed. Thanks to the random draw, I would be the final performer. My bladder ached with the urge to pee, but I'd already gone to the bathroom five times. Ms. Whitaker strolled back onto the stage.

"Aren't these ladies talented, y'all?! I wish they all could be Melva's Miss Livermush! Well, we have two more girls left, both from Melva High School. Up next, we have Margo Werther, who will be singing, and she will immediately be followed by our final performer, Janice Wills!"

The crowd cheered. I watched Margo walk out onto the stage again. She wore the same green dress she'd been wearing, but now she'd added a huge gardenia placed in her hair, like Billie Holiday. The audience grew hushed; Margo had presence.

She leaned in to the microphone. I waited for some sort of tinny music to begin over the loudspeakers, but nothing played. Silence. And then, finally, she began to sing unaccompanied.

She sang "Amazing Grace," an atypical pageant song, perhaps, but the crowd listened in awed silence. Margo's voice, a warm, rich contralto, flowed over them. My neck prickled at "how sweet the sound." My arms were goose-bumped again. I watched Margo's back onstage as she swayed slightly, prolonging the notes. Even without my glasses, I could tell the crowd was transfixed, hanging on her every syllable. Margo was annihilating the rest of the competition.

When she held the quavering final note to its finish, nothing happened. For a few moments, everyone was completely still. There were no "Whoo-hoo! That's my girl!" no whistles, no nothing. People started clapping as if hesitant, made shy by Margo's performance. The clapping grew slowly, and then it was thunderous. The crowd was on their feet. They began to whistle and cheer. Someone, an old man, shouted, "Bravo! Encore!"

Margo bowed slightly. The clapping continued and continued. Finally Ms. Whitaker had to step onstage and motion for silence.

"Ahem. Great, yes, beautiful. And now, for our final performer, Janice Wills!"

I walked quickly to the center of the stage. How could I follow Margo? And how could I follow Margo with this:

"Hi, ev-everyone. My name is Janice Wills, and for my talent, I will be reading an essay entitled 'Margaret Mead, Manners, and Melva: An Anthropologist Comes of Age in the Land of Livermush.' "

The crowd gazed at me silently. This, I noted, was a different silence from the one Margo had encountered. Someone coughed. My title had seemed so clever on my computer screen at home five months ago, but now — oh, well. I needed to begin:

"The esteemed anthropologist Margaret Mead once said, 'Anthropology demands the open-mindedness with which one must look and listen, record in astonishment, and wonder that which one would not have been able to guess.' I have felt that growing up in Melva has taught me to look and listen carefully, and certainly to record in astonishment. Melva citizens celebrate a heavily spiced pork product over sculpture or painting. The locus of cultural activity is often the Super Wal-Mart parking lot. A seasonal sporting event involving muscled high school males charging against one another in helmets holds near-religious ritual significance. Instead of literary salons, we have only beauty salons. As a result, some might say that Melva is a town full of small-minded, provincial individuals. Some might say this town is very boring. . . ."

I paused to take a gulp of air. Had my paper sounded so snobby back when I'd first written it? It was becoming clear to me that this was the worst idea of my life. Months ago, my words had sounded smart. Sophisticated. Why did I now sound like a brat? I could see audience members staring at me like I was covered in green scales. I cleared my throat and straightened my pages.

Someone shouted, "Reading an essay's not a talent! Boring!"

"Shut up!" a woman shouted. "Shut your stupid face and be polite!"

The shouting grew louder and indistinguishable. I froze for a moment, unsure what to do. There was no way I could read the rest of this paper. I cleared my throat again and began to speak off the cuff.

"Ummm. I'm just going to talk, y'all. Not read . . . So anyway, that's what people often think. People *who do not take the time to get to know Melva, that is.* People who have not always stopped to observe Melva *truly* with the open-mindedness that Margaret Mead mentions." I coughed, then coughed again, my mouth gone dry. "Melva is made up of people, wonderful people. Take my neighbor, Mrs. Crandor — there's no one friendlier! Or Stephen Shepherd, who's going to be the world's next major innovator in aeronautics; or my friends Tanesha and Susannah, who are not only two of the best dancers in the entire state but also two of the most patient teachers; or Mr. Thompson, who runs the local ice-cream shop and takes the time to keep up with what's going on in the lives of his customers; or my incredibly talented best friend, Margo, who just sang for y'all — you heard her! Amazing. All right here in Melva. And there are many more, so many more. . . ."

I looked out into the crowd. My mom shot me a thumbs-up. I realized at this point that my eyes were tearing up, and I felt like a politician on the news trying to make amends after a faux pas. But I meant it. I meant every word, and so I kept talking.

"I love so many people in this town. I'm appreciative. And like everyone here, I'm learning — learning to look and listen, just as Margaret Mead suggested. We are all learning, changing, making mistakes and faltering at times but always learning —"

That's when the microphone and all the stage lights went out. There was a huge blare of speaker feedback that startled everyone. The crowd gasped. I tapped the microphone, shaking a little. Nothing. I looked around for help, for Ms. Whitaker or Blair or someone.

The crowd was growing anxious. I could hear their collective murmuring grow like distant thunder.

"The esteemed anthropologist Margaret Mead taught me —" I began again. The microphone was completely dead. I tried once more, shouting, "THE ESTEEMED ANTHROPOLOGIST MARGARET MEAD TAUGHT ME —"

I looked over at Ms. Whitaker, but she didn't seem to understand that the sound wasn't working. She raised her eyebrows and gestured for me to go on.

There was no way I could shout my essay out to the audience. My mom just kept smiling up at me and waving. I squinted at her — her big, Bisquick biscuit of a face all made up and beaming. And then, inspiration struck.

I started doing the Pony.

I skipped to the left-two-three. I skipped to the right, holding my fists forward the way my mom had. It was so quiet that I could hear my feet thumping on the stage. I hummed an old soul song to myself for inspiration. And amazingly, I felt good — silly, happy, pleased with good ol' Melva and with myself.

"It's the Pony!" some middle-aged woman who was not my mom shouted. "All right, girl! Do the Pony! All right!"

"Get it, girl! Work it!" another lady shouted, then started clapping. A few people started laughing, but their laughter seemed supportive, the kind of laughter that felt like it was rooting me on. I almost burst out laughing myself.

When Ms. Whitaker finally came out onto the stage to lead me off, the audience applauded (and possibly looked a little relieved). But my mom stayed on her feet, cheering. And cheering.

ANTHROPOLOGICAL
OBSERVATION #20:

I will simply agree with the following Margaret Mead quotation: "I have a respect for manners as such, they are a way of dealing with people you don't agree with or like."

I was still shaking when Margo clutched my arm in the wings. "Wow! You had a real change-of-heart moment up there, huh?" Margo whispered, grinning at me.

I shook my head, still lost in a sort of haze. "Was it okay?" I asked.

"Seriously great while it lasted. You handled it brilliantly," she said, throwing her arms around me. "Especially when you threw in the Pony."

But before we could talk anymore, Ms. Whitaker hushed everyone, gathering all of us finalists together into the greenroom.

"Girls, we believe we have addressed the problem with our sound board. Y'all will now each do your interviews. Afterward, the judges will make their final decisions."

The other girls broke into murmurs, either distressed or appreciative. I was swept with a wave of relief that I wouldn't have to reattempt reading my essay. There was no way that I wanted to go back on that stage to repeat that talent. Answering interview questions would be less stressful by comparison.

Ms. Whitaker continued. "Finally, as planned, we will reconvene after the interviews at six p.m., for the awards announcements and ceremony."

With that, Ms. Whitaker left, and Blair passed out the interview schedule, ushering the first girl on the list back out to the stage. The rest of us clustered near the curtains, watching, listening to the answers.

"What would you say your greatest weakness is?" one judge asked into the microphone.

The first girl approached the mike hesitantly, as if it might shock her. "My greatest weakness," she said faintly, "is probably that I work too hard. I become too invested in things and never give up. It can be a lot of stress when you're so dedicated. People say to me, 'Just relax a little!' but I always have to respond, 'No. I can't. I care too much, and so I have to keep working.' That's my greatest weakness."

The first girl left, and another girl walked onto the stage.

"Lord Acton once said, 'Power corrupts; and absolute power corrupts absolutely.' How do you respond to this claim?"

"This is an absolutely powerful statement," the next girl said, "because power is very corrupting, as we may see in Stalinist Russia, where there was both much corruption and power, and the super-complicated relationship between both, which leads to corruption in an absolute sense. So absolutely this is absolutely true."

I had no idea what the girl had just said, but the audience clapped politely.

TR went out next.

"Some say that our greatest problems are our greatest opportunities. Do you agree with this statement and why?"

TR answered, "I've been taught by many mentors, including Oprah Winfrey and my mother, to look at the greatest problems as the greatest opportunities. The example that comes to my mind is when the members of the cheerleading squad did not have enough new cheerleading uniforms for everyone. Instead of viewing this as a problem, I said, 'Hey, this is an opportunity. Why don't we seek donations from all our parents, and instead of just getting enough for the missing uniforms, we'll have an opportunity to get nice new uniforms for everyone!' And that's how we ended up with cute new uniforms for the entire squad. And thus I truly believe all great problems are actually just opportunities in disguise."

I had to swallow my own vomit on that one. After TR, the rest of the interview questions went by in a blur. Finally it was my turn. I walked out onstage.

"What piece of advice would you like to give to a young girl who might be standing exactly where you're standing ten years from now?"

I thought for a minute. Bring extra bobby pins? Make sure you have on strong deodorant? Don't let your mom pick out your Miss Livermush dress? Then I remembered what my mom had said to me. It now seemed like she'd definitely been onto something.

"Try to remember," I said, "that it's difficult to have any perspective on things when you're sixteen or seventeen. And difficult sometimes to appreciate the people and things around you. So try to be generous to yourself and others."

What a dork I sounded like. What clichéd and stupid-sounding advice! My heart was still pounding as I walked offstage. But the more I thought about it, the more I reassured myself that nothing I'd said was untrue. I'd made a good point, really — my mom's good point. But how much easier to say than to execute in real life.

• • •

When we'd finished our interviews and changed into regular clothes, my mom was the only mother waiting outside the Arts Council building on her tiptoes, periodically jumping up and down. My dad stood beside her, shuffling his feet and looking off to the side, almost as if he were embarrassed to be next to a giddy, jumping, middle-aged woman wearing a "LIVERMUSH, THE GREATEST STUFF!!!" T-shirt.

"Oh, Miss Livermush, Miss Livermush!" she chirped, jumping up and down while Margo and I walked out. "You were both so beautiful, girls! I'm so proud! You're all winners in my book!"

FACT:
My mom was the type of person who could say things like "You're all winners in my book!" and be absolutely sincere about it.

"Did I look dumb, Mom? When the microphone cut out?" I whispered to her as she hugged me.

"Don't be silly," my mom said. "It made you look very poised, I thought, the way you handled it with such good humor! I thought to myself, those old judges are saying, *That girl has* incredible *poise!*"

"Thanks, Mom," I said, hugging her tighter.

"Chucky Healey's mother was sitting next to me, and she said you just looked beautiful!"

I pulled myself back, looked at my mom, and groaned.

Then my mom looked at me seriously. "I heard what you were saying up there, Janice. Before the microphone went out. I liked where you were going. Your father and I are very proud of you."

My dad nodded at me like we'd just made a business deal together.

"You're my princess," he said for the hundredth time, as if this finally made it so.

"Thanks, Dad," I said, before my mom pulled me into a hug again.

· · ·

After I disentangled myself from my mother's five-minute-long Bear Hug of Pageant Enthusiasm, and I managed to convince her that she didn't need to hang out with us at the festival, Margo and I went to walk around on our own. We had a few hours to spend before the awards ceremony.

The afternoon had grown less cloudy, and the Livermush Festival was now bustling. We headed past face painting stands and French fry stands, stands representing local businesses, and of course, livermush stands: livermush biscuits, fried livermush, livermush and cheese. Tired-looking women waddled along in shorts, screeching at their little kids, who zipped around, keyed up on sugar, grease, and face paint. Middle schoolers and high school freshmen passed by in little clusters. Local businessmen and Realtor-types clasped one another's hands firmly and slapped one another on the back. Aside from the Letherfordton County Fair, this was the biggest community social event of the year. Everyone in Melva who could be out was out, and the air smelled thick and greasy with livermush frying. The livermush air clung to our nostrils and clothes as we walked. Margo and I walked slowly, absorbing it all. I liked this smell, I thought. I liked its familiarity.

Then we noticed a crowd of people our age in the parking lot behind the Arts building. Margo and I walked closer. There were a bunch of trucks parked there. Guys in backward trucker caps milled around, and several bare-legged girls hung out on the truck beds. A couple of the guys were drinking from bottles of Mountain Dew that I guessed had something else mixed in. Many of them held another soda bottle into which they'd spit periodically. There was a lot of chasing and squealing and flirting, new girls strolling up in packs and showing off their lean, bare legs in miniskirts. I didn't recognize most of them and so assumed they were county kids. Except for TR and her crew.

TR and her crew were still wearing their Miss Livermush gowns, and (now that I was an expert in the matter) they appeared to be tipsy. Laughing and falling against one another, the three girls climbed into the back of a big red truck with an "I brake for boiled peanuts" bumper sticker. They waved Margo and me over.

"Hey, hey! Nice dancing up there, Janice!" TR said, giggling a little.

"So what are y'all up to?" Margo asked, ignoring TR's comment.

Tabitha hiccupped. Casey gave a squealing little laugh.

"We're sssslirting," Casey said, breaking into a squeal again.

"Slirting!" TR said. "Slirting."

"Oh, wow," Margo whispered to me. "This is for real. For some reason, I always thought they were exaggerating."

TR cackled, jumping in. "Normally we go to a really crappy place like the Rutherville Quik-Stop or the Wal-Mart parking lot!" She grinned. "But today with the Livermush Festival going on, they come right to us!"

ANTHROPOLOGIST'S NOTE:
Rutherville was one of the few places people in Melva felt confident mocking, as it was even smaller and perceived to be even more "country" than Melva itself. If you lived in Melva, you felt you were allowed to make incest and moonshine jokes about Rutherville.

Margo and I exchanged a look.

"Isn't that, sort of, I dunno — evil?" I asked.

The three girls cackled drunkenly.

"No, no, no! They love it! They love that we're paying attention to them, and they never know that we think they're really complete losers!" Casey said.

"The girls get mad, though," TR added wisely, with a hint of glee. "Like today. Those county girls hate us!"

"You're invading their turf," Margo said. "And mocking their friends."

"Whatever!" Tabitha squealed. "They're total rednecks! We're, like, the thrill of their chaw-chewin' lives!"

"Yeah! And these aren't even the worst we've ever tried. They're, like, awesome compared to some of the guys we've found!" Casey added.

As if to demonstrate, TR practically jumped onto the lap of a nearby guy in a camouflage hat. He looked up, startled but not disappointed. TR took a swig of his drink, and then, grabbing his neck, she lifted his face up to hers and kissed him. It was a full, slow, long kiss. Margo and I stared, speechless.

When their lips finally disconnected, the guy looked up, bewildered and pleased, at TR. With that, she sprang back and slapped him in the face. Hard. The sound of the slap was loud enough that everyone turned.

"What the —" the guy began. One half of his face was red, and his eyes glistened like he might be holding back tears.

"What do you think you're doing, kissing someone like me?" TR hissed. "Where do you even get the nerve?"

"Not cool, TR," I said. She turned to face me, her eyes fierce and feline.

Margo looked at me, her brow furrowed. "What do we do?" she whispered.

"I don't know," I said. "Let's just get out of here."

• • •

We quickly walked back to the main area of the festival, right around the court square. While Margo ran inside the courthouse to use the bathroom, I stood waiting by a frozen lemonade stand, idly inspecting my fingernails. I sensed a person approaching me and looked up.

"Excuse me," he mumbled, stepping back before I'd even registered who he was. He smelled of cigarettes and peppermint chewing gum. He wore dark jeans and a black shirt.

Jimmy Denton.

He scowled — not at me, it seemed, but as if he were trying to pluck the right words from the air.

"Hey," I said. "I didn't see you." Which was a stupid thing to say since of course I hadn't seen him until he'd walked right up to me.

He shrugged, scratching his head behind one ear and just staring at me. Quiet. A sour taste rose in my throat. I thought of Mrs. Johnson's whistling old voice spitting near my ear during the fancy walking lessons. I thought of my mom's advice. I thought of the night at Jimmy's.

"You know," I said. "What you did that night, how you acted to me, it wasn't cool. It wasn't cool at all. I'm sorry that you've had a rough time in this town, but you're not the only one."

He stared at me, unblinking. He was the cutest guy I'd ever seen, and yet he looked ugly to me. No, not ugly. Just unappealing.

"A nice person, a *decent* person, would apologize," I said. My voice was dropping quieter and quieter for some reason, until I was only barely audible. "And if *you* are having problems, maybe you should TALK to someone. Don't just be bitter and mean. Especially to people who want to like you."

Jimmy cleared his throat but said nothing.

"And I liked you. I wanted to get to know you," I said, looking right into his eyes.

But he still didn't say a word, just shuffled one of his dirty shoes a little, as if he were wiping away a spot on the ground.

"I was going to tell you . . ." he said, then paused. "I was going to say . . ."

"Listen, don't worry about it," I said. "We're cool. I've moved on."

And, as an Anthropologist/Reluctant Participant in Livermush Pageants and also a newly minted Woman of Action, I think I really *had* moved on. I turned from Jimmy and walked away.

ANTHROPOLOGICAL
OBSERVATION #21:

The threat of mutual destruction is a strong deterrent and may ensure a temporary peace between rival factions.

At 5:55 p.m., we were back in our dresses and waiting in the wings again. The translucent powder I wore was barely preventing my whole face from dripping with sweat. My clenched hands were cool and damp, like balled-up athletic socks.

The audience had gathered again, and this time there were more of them. At 5:59, you could feel every atom of our bodies backstage buzzing with anticipation. I squeezed Margo's hand behind me.

FACT:

I had realized that, in spite of it all, I secretly hoped I might win — maybe not first place, but second. Third, even. Maybe, just maybe, the judges had found my answer to the interview question mind-blowing. I wanted Margo to do well too, but I'd realized it was easier to wish your best friend well when she wasn't obviously about to trounce you in a contest.

Ms. Whitaker, covered in her geological layers of foundation, walked back onstage, greeted by loud applause.

"Good evening, everyone, and welcome back to the awards ceremony for this year's Melva's Miss Livermush! After much deliberation, the judges have reached their decision."

The crowd clapped. Someone wolf-whistled.

"Now I'd like to ask all our finalists back onto the stage. As you know, this is more than a pageant; it is also a scholarship competition. We are proud of every one of these young ladies, but there may be only one Miss Livermush."

A recorded drumroll blared over the crappy replacement sound system.

"This year, the judges would first like to award a prize for outstanding accomplishment in the academic portion of the competition. This year's winner wrote what was deemed to be the best essay on the subject of livermush as well. The winner this year of the academic prize is . . . Janice Wills!"

Margo gasped and squeezed my hand, pushing me forward. *A nerd prize*, I couldn't help thinking. The judges must have felt sorry for the interruption during my talent. I stood under the lights, stunned and uncertain as a newborn baby mole, blinking into the applauding audience as Ms. Whitaker handed me a sash and bouquet.

"This year's second runner-up . . . we are proud to announce . . . is Jessica Robertson!"

As Jessica, a girl from the county high school, accepted her flowers, tears slid down her cheeks — tears that I suspected Jessica hoped looked like tears of happiness. My guess was that they were not, but that she would recover and be genuinely happy soon enough.

"Our first runner-up this year, the young lady who will fill in for Miss Livermush should it be required, is the lovely and talented . . . Theresa Rose Venable!"

Tabitha and Casey crowed happily above the applause. TR, blond hair shimmering, hugged Ms. Whitaker and took her bouquet. I focused on maintaining my own smile, focused on the pain this smile was now causing my facial muscles.

"Finally, after her dazzling talent performance, we are pleased to crown Margo Werther as MELVA'S MISS LIVERMUSH!"

Margo rushed forward, and the crowd rose to their feet clapping. "You Are So Beautiful" again blasted out from the speaker system. Ms. Whitaker hugged us each again, giving us air-kisses on each cheek. I felt a little light-headed.

After the applause had died down, Jessica, Margo, TR, and I were swept backstage on a tide of congratulations from the other girls. Still, I heard a few sniffles.

"Wonderful, wonderful!" Ms. Whitaker gushed, following us. "We're proud of you all this year, and especially of our three scholarship recipients."

I knew I should be pleased. I hadn't gotten a scholarship, but I did receive a $500 check for the academic prize.

After the congratulations died down, all of us began gathering up our stuff. Girls chatted with one another quietly, everyone sounding more subdued than before the pageant had started. But when I heard Margo's voice begin to rise, I turned around. Her voice had grown so loud that everyone was watching.

Margo and TR stood facing each other, both of them still in their formal dresses. Margo was shaking a brush right in TR's face.

" . . . but you are the most manipulative, evil, selfish . . . I CARE about him, and NOTHING bad was going on, and now YOU are going to get him in trouble!"

Margo's face was sweaty. Wet threads of mascara ran down her face.

"Listen, Margo, Miss Livermush Princess Whatever," TR said. "I don't effing CARE about what you do with your SLUTTY self. But the Livermush judges just might! Remember 'excellent moral character'? Remember that from the guidelines?"

Margo shook her head angrily. We were all staring unabashedly now, all of us other girls in our dresses forming an anticipatory circle of eyes. I could tell everyone's breath was held, waiting for the real fight to break out.

ANTHROPOLOGIST'S NOTE:

According to my survey, it is the prevailing opinion among male adolescents in Melva that fights between females, or "girl fights," are far more interesting and far meaner than the male equivalent. And everyone likes watching them. Primary source quotation: "Dude! And then Kiki, like, ripped this chunk of hair off Jessica's head, and there was, like, still flesh attached! And all of us watching were like, 'Dude, this girl fight is *awesome!*' "

I grabbed Margo's shoulder, pulling her toward me.

"What's going on?" I hissed. "What's this about?"

TR, stalking toward us, heard me.

"Oh, you didn't know either, did you, Janice? Margo's kept us all in the dark, even her dear little best friend," TR said. Her voice was sweet and toxic.

I looked at Margo, who didn't meet my eyes.

"What's she talking about?" I asked. "What?"

"Oh, just the fact that she's been dating Colin. The FreshLife leader. Which is totally against every single rule," TR said gleefully.

"Colin the FreshLife leader?" I whisper-hissed at Margo, feeling all the eyes in the room on us. "He's Secret Boyfriend? Are you serious?"

Margo fiddled with a seam on her dress, still not meeting my eyes. My head pounded. I couldn't tell if I was angrier at the thought of Margo paired with Colin or at the fact that Margo hadn't told me this huge secret. And I, her best friend . . .

"Janice, he's, like, two years older than we are," Margo whispered. "And I didn't mean for it to happen, but . . . I liked him. He liked me. And I couldn't tell you even though I wanted to! He made me promise — and I didn't want to get him in trouble!"

I sighed.

"I feel morally bound," TR said loudly, "as someone of *excellent* moral character, to make this piece of information known to the Miss Livermush judges. It is explicitly against FreshLife rules, after all! This might make them rethink their decision."

I looked at Margo. Her face was awash in streaky mascara, her mouth a rictus of panic. How could TR have possibly found out this piece of information before I had? It gnawed at my gut. But I looked at TR, her devilish Barbie face still gleeful, and I knew I had to act.

"Well, TR," I said carefully and loud enough for the whole room to hear, "if we're going to be complete about it, there are other things the judges might be interested in. Like, for instance, *slirting*. Like, for instance, drinking underage behind the Arts Council building in the middle of the Livermush Festival. Like, for instance, slapping some poor guy in the face."

I thought of my anthropology notes at home — of all the times I'd observed TR and her group laughing viciously in the face of some dumpy guy who'd previously believed that he was successfully flirting. Actually I had plenty of notes involving TR laughing in the faces of many people, male and female, whether slirting or not.

TR blinked at me. "What? No. I mean . . ."

"Slirting. Consumption of alcohol underage *during* the pageant. Really, when it comes to lapses in moral character . . . You name it. In fact, I probably have more anthropological notes on these subjects at home. The judges might be very interested in learning more."

Some of the girls in the room looked confused. I heard them whisper the word "slirting" with question marks in their voices. The murmuring grew behind me. I stared hard, unrelentingly, at TR.

I paused for a moment, then added, "If I'm wrong, I'm sure the Melva police department would be happy to let you prove your innocence with one of their Breathalyzers."

She looked at me and shook her head. "Whatever, Janice. Forget it, okay? If you wanna be a brat about something — about NOTHING, really — then just forget it." And with that, she stalked out of the room, trailed by Casey and Tabitha.

I felt Margo shudder with relief beside me.

"Janice," she whispered, touching my arm. "Thank you."

I took a breath, absorbing the fact that I'd actually stood down TR — and that I'd used my anthropological powers to do it.

"Of course," I said, hugging her. "But you have a lot to catch me up on."

ANTHROPOLOGICAL OBSERVATION #22:

In many cultures, the sexualized nature of certain dances is perceived as a threat to the social order; but often, it is not the dancing but rather peripheral social intrigues that lead to trouble.

And so I like to think I saved the day. The observations of the anthropologist, when applied appropriately, can preempt a situation from spiraling further out of control. I was using my critical powers for Good, not Evil. Plus when it came to documenting the pageant for the sake of anthropology, I realized something else:

ANTHROPOLOGIST'S NOTE:

It becomes far more difficult to be anthropologically detached from something once you receive an award for it — even if you're not sure how you feel about receiving that award. Instead you sort of feel like, "Hey, yeah, sure — if you'd like to honor me, I'll take that honor. Maybe you're right!" Perhaps this is why Cortez did not set the record straight when he was mistaken for the returning god, Quetzalcoatl, by the Aztecs. Okay, it probably also helped Cortez conquer them and steal their gold, but still. You get the point. It's cool to be given awards (even nerd prizes) or to be mistaken for a god.

The person who took the greatest pleasure in my academic award was, yes, my mom. Everyone had dispersed home for a few hours before the Livermush Festival Dance, and my mom assaulted me the moment I'd walked into the kitchen.

"Sweetheart! Janice! You did it!" she shouted, running up to hug me.

"Thanks, Mom," I said. "But it's not really a big deal."

She looked at me, and her eyes started to get a little teary. She took me in her arms again. It made me feel like the academic award was actually something important, not just a nerd prize.

"No," she whispered. "It is a big deal. You deserved it. You were wonderful."

And I hugged my mom for a long time, and considered the fact that even though she a) was obsessed with Kenny G-ified versions of '80s pop songs b) now had on a red shirt with an appliquéd chunk of anthropomorphic livermush on it (yes, the livermush had eyes and was smiling) and c) believed in doing Jazzercise-based mall aerobics, she was a darn good mom.

"Thanks, Mom," I said. "I never thought I'd say this, but I almost don't regret the fact that you encouraged me to do this."

And then, just in case she thought I was getting too soft and mushy, I added, "But Mom, your shirt! It's hurting me! It's actually physically painful to behold!"

Without seeming embarrassed at all, my mom broke into a little burst of the Pony. The little livermush googly eyes jiggled back and forth on her torso.

"My shirt is fabulous," she said, still smiling. So perhaps, in some ways of perceiving the universe, my mom is unassailably awesome.

• • •

The Livermush Dance felt like a relief after the stress of the Livermush Pageant itself. I figured at this point, now that I'd demonstrated my dance moves before an entire audience, the dance floor itself would be relatively low pressure.

Margo was anxious about showing up now that people knew she'd been seeing Colin — even though the TR disaster had been averted.

"You think I should go?" she asked.

"Of course. You ARE Miss Livermush."

"But I'm humiliated. I don't know. I —"

"Trust me," I said. "It'll be much more of a big deal if you don't show up."

"And Janice, I got in touch with Colin. TR found out because Colin told the FreshLife advisor. He stepped down from his position."

"To be with you?" I asked. "Really?"

"I don't know," Margo said. "I don't know. I think he felt like it was the right thing to do regardless, and we do like each other.

But we're just gonna take it slowly, see what happens. It's been too complicated. Right now it's just a relief not to have to keep something a big secret."

"Then don't worry about it anymore! At least not for now!" I said.

"It's still embarrassing," Margo said. "And I can't believe you found out that way. I wanted to tell you when he and I first went out to the movies the other week, and then we finally kissed, and I was just *dying* to tell. I — I'm just embarrassed now that everyone will know."

"Margo, it's okay! I'm happy for you! So you kissed the FreshLife leader. The former FreshLife leader. So you guys went to the movies. We're almost seventeen. He's nineteen. It's a blurry issue anyway, and the issue has been addressed for now. Let's just go to this dance and celebrate the fact that you are the new official Melva's Miss Livermush. Okay?"

"You're sure?" Margo asked.

"Yes," I said. "About everything. And especially about this dance. You know the theme is 'This Magic Moment,' right? It's going to be awesome, and by *awesome*, I mean cheesy and fantastic."

Margo squeezed my shoulder. Smiling, she said, "All right, Ms. Optimistic. Let's go."

• • •

When we got to the dance, mostly the dorks were there — some of the Formerly Homeschooled and some of the Bleakest Geek couples. Apparently they'd wanted to seize This Magic Moment early. One couple had come in Star Wars gear with light sabers. A few Chess Nerds and even one or two of the Smart Pretties and their dates followed. A tight cluster of Evangelical-But-Not-Antidancing-Evangelical Christian kids were talking in same-sex clusters, wearing their demure, body-concealing formal attire. By the time the DJ tried to play "The Electric Slide," enough Baseball Guys and Cool Black Girls had shown up that everyone was able to boo the DJ into changing his selection. Middle-aged parents and community members slow-danced right next to teenaged couples. A few old people fox-trotted around the room. Another version of myself would have found the overall picture strange and weird and discomfiting, but for some reason, tonight it seemed, well, *nice*. Like everyone was just happy to be together and have a good time.

When we got to the dance floor, Margo and I began dancing self-consciously in a tight girl clump. I held my arms stiff at my sides until Tanesha walked over and offered a little coaching.

"Move your arms, Janice. *Lève les bras! Les bras!*" she shouted, breaking into giggles. "Remember the dance steps I taught you!"

She started the routine, and I joined her. And at this point, friends, I was officially dancing. Not the Pony — legit break-it-down dancing. And I confess to you: It was fun.

About an hour and a half into things, I noticed TR, Jimmy, Tabitha, and Tripp walk inside. TR and Tabitha of course looked like they belonged on a red carpet somewhere. Their long dresses were sapphire blue and cherry red, respectively.

TR glided over, dancing her way within earshot of Margo. Margo stiffened but kept dancing. I moved protectively toward her. Jimmy stood nearby, un-dancing, but drumming his fingers against the wall. He looked away from us.

"Hey!" TR called over the music. "Miss Livermush! Been having any more forbidden love affairs? Punching guys in the face? Vomiting on people's shoes? You know — your specialties?"

Margo whipped around. TR blinked benignly with her large, lovely eyes. She had a lily corsage on her slender wrist. Expensive and exotic. Wordlessly Margo grabbed the lily and calmly tore it to delicate, tiny bits, which she let flutter onto the dance floor.

ANTHROPOLOGIST'S NOTE:

Once again, we see an impetuous, solitary act of aggression perpetrated against a leader of the stronger tribe, in this case perhaps deliberately intended to signify a refusal to cave to future efforts at domination. I.e. this was an act of rebellion, however irrational. (Although as an aside, this anthropologist must ask, "Margo, what were you thinking?!")

Immediately Margo locked terrified eyes with me. We both knew it was exactly the wrong thing to have done. Tanesha and I stopped dancing completely. TR stepped forward, muttering angrily. I looked up and caught Jimmy's eyes. Jimmy caught TR by the arm.

"Come on, Theresa Rose. Forget it. Let's go over here," he said.

TR gave Margo a seething look one more time. "You think you're so good, Margo Werther, but you're not. You and Janice too. You're not all good and sweet and nice. You're just like everybody else here, even though you pretend you're not."

And with that, TR turned and let Jimmy lead her away. This was far from the meanest thing TR had ever said to us, but for some reason it struck me the most — because I realized there was some truth to it.

I wiped my forehead, heading over to the refreshments table for another glass of punch. When I returned to the dance floor, Margo and I were incorporated into a dance circle with Tanesha Jones and a couple of her friends.

ANTHROPOLOGIST'S NOTE:
As in most traditional cultures, the modern American adolescent dances predominately in group circles, at least during fast songs. Periodically, the ritual is to urge one person into the center of the circle with chants of "Go, Janice! Go, Janice! Go, Janice!" whereupon the nominated individual must perform some amazing solo dance moves, or, if you are nerdy like me, resort to nerd-hipster standby dances like the Lawn Mower or the Sprinkler.

Aside from the awkward moment with TR, Margo seemed to be having a blast, and so was I. The key to dancing, I decided,

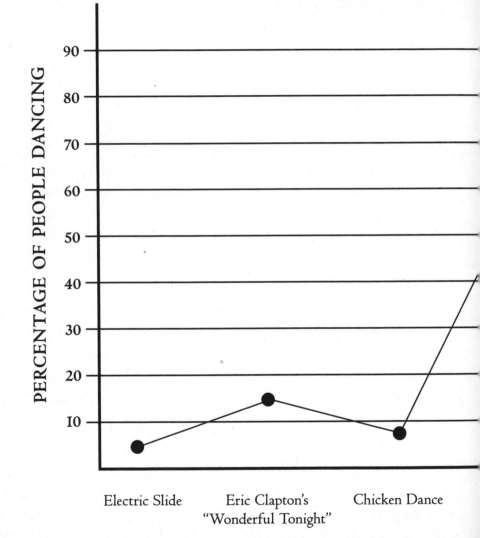

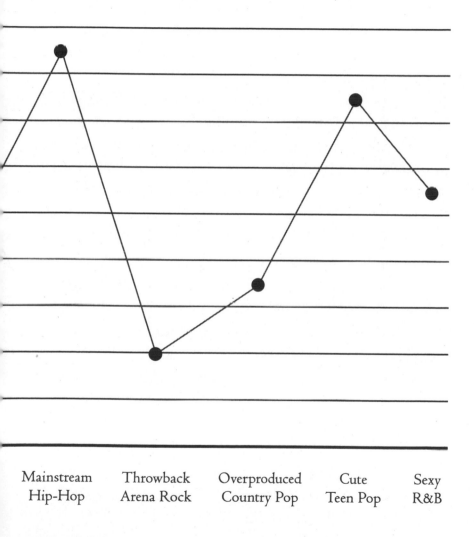

LIVERMUSH FESTIVAL

DANCE POPULATION VIS-A-VIS MUSIC SELECTIONS

Mainstream Hip-Hop	Throwback Arena Rock	Overproduced Country Pop	Cute Teen Pop	Sexy R&B

SELECTIONS

was making many exaggerated facial expressions, thereby embracing your own ridiculousness. I was impressed by our dancing. I was also impressed by my hair: Although I was sweaty and exhausted, my hair had not budged an inch. That was the power of my mom's industrial-strength hair spray reinforced by two handfuls of bobby pins. (I probably wouldn't wear that much hair spray again until my wedding, but this seemed very low on my list of present worries.)

In my peripheral vision, I kept noticing Jimmy Denton. He lurked along the edges of the dance floor, weaving his way among the tables where a few of the Bleakest Geeks were cemented to their seats. He hadn't danced at all. TR had returned to the dance floor, and she, Tabitha, Casey, and about seven other girls seemed to be desperately throwing themselves into their own performance of No One Has Fun Like We Do! They danced and lip-synched and acted out the songs in their circle in a way that suggested that, if you were not among them, you might as well go home and watch infomercials and cry. They were good at this. TR's unadorned wrist and her proximity to Margo made me a little nervous.

After a few more songs, Margo disappeared. When she came back, her face was scrunched with worry. She pulled me a little closer to TR and her crew. When TR saw us, she looked up, caught sight of Margo, and snarled. I looked at her upturned, pastel lips with horror.

"Theresa Rose, can I talk to you for a minute?" Margo yelled. A particularly loud song was blaring.

"I can't hear you. I'm dancing." TR swung her head, and a lash of blond hair whipped Margo in the mouth.

"CAN I TALK TO YOU?"

I nudged Margo on the arm and gave her a look. What was she doing?

"WHY WOULD I WANT TO TALK TO YOU?" TR shouted back and held up her bare wrist meaningfully. She turned around, flinging her arms to the music with new ferocity. Margo huffed and stalked over to the nearest table. I followed her. She plopped down in an empty chair, and we watched TR gyrate with her friends.

"What were you trying to do?" I asked, studying her.

Margo puffed air out of her mouth, blowing a wisp of hair from her eyes. "I wanted to apologize," she said. "Believe it or not. It was stupid, what I did to her corsage. And I wanted to tell her she did a nice job in the pageant, and tell her sorry about how the whole night at the party went, and that I just wanted to get along."

"Oh, man . . ." I said. "Still, she's acted pretty lame. And the whole slirting thing is extremely lame."

"I know," Margo said. "We'll see if she keeps slirting after today. But regardless. I need to apologize."

"Here," Jimmy said, appearing suddenly and tapping Margo on the shoulder. He stood behind us, looking half-cocky, half-shy, with something in his hand. It was a flower made of paper — and it was beautiful. The petals were full and multicolored. He handed it to Margo. She looked closer, touching it with her index finger.

"Wow," she breathed. "Where'd you get this?"

He shrugged. "I made it," he said. "It's an apology flower." He turned from Margo and looked pointedly at me.

Margo held the flower closer for me to see as well. It was pieced together out of napkins and streamers.

"You're really good," Margo said admiringly. "Isn't he, Janice?"

"Yeah," I said, puzzling over his face.

"It's nothing. I don't like to dance really, so I've gotta keep myself occupied somehow." He paused. "I saw you out there with TR. I thought it might help if you gave her this. You know, a replacement for the other one. It won't go on her wrist, but she could pin it to her dress."

Margo smiled at him. "Thanks," she said. "That's really thoughtful. I'll go take it to her now."

With her hands full of the intricately folded paper flower, Margo walked back out to TR. She walked gingerly, as if the apology were an actual physical object — complicated, impromptu, delicate, like the replacement corsage flower in her hands.

Jimmy still stood near me, so close that I could hear him breathing. I kept my eyes on Margo so that I wouldn't have to look at him.

"Oh, and I made one for you too," he said, handing me another paper flower. The delicate petals trembled. Jimmy's hand was shaking.

"I —" he started. "About that night . . . I . . . it's been a rough year, a rough couple years, and I . . ."

I held up my hand. "No, it's okay," I said. "Thank you for this."

He looked relieved.

"And you were right," I added. "I did read your blog — before your party. I was curious about you, so I Googled you and found it. I should have just said so when you asked. For what it's worth, I thought it was good. You're an interesting guy."

"Thanks. You're interesting too, Janice."

I smiled at him — even though I knew my teeth were now red from the punch.

"Good luck next year, Jimmy," I said.

"Yeah, you too."

He turned and walked away, and I considered the possibility that maybe people like Jimmy and me were going to turn out all right after all.

ANTHROPOLOGICAL
OBSERVATION #23:

Classical comedies usually culminate in marriage. For the American adolescent, the social dramedy usually culminates at a dance.

I watched Jimmy disappear into the sweaty crowd. I held the paper flower he'd given me.

ANTHROPOLOGIST'S NOTE:
Gifts of contrition are important parts of apology rituals in many cultures. For instance, for a ritual apology in Fiji, the apologizer may offer *tabua*, or sperm whale teeth, as a rare and precious gift.

ADDITIONAL NOTE:
Margaret Mead once said, "Always remember that you are absolutely unique. Just like everyone else." This quotation had always sort of depressed me. Tonight it was oddly reassuring.

When the next song began, I rose from my seat and found my friends on the dance floor. I tried to pin the flower to my strap, but it wouldn't stay put while I danced.

NOTE TO THE ANTHROPOLOGIST'S MOTHER IF SHE EVER READS THIS:

I *knew* these discount dresses were a terrible idea! Even with this non-terrible one chosen by Margo and me and Berneatha, the straps would not stick to my skinny shoulders, and now that I was dancing like crazy (dancing in a way that would make you, Mom, beam with pride, if you could actually see me from where all the older people are hanging out on the other side of the Elks' Lodge), I couldn't keep the darn thing up. Every five seconds, I found myself hiking the dress up so my bird-chest nipples didn't spring greetings onto the world.

Despite the dress, I admit: I was having fun.

Just then, someone grabbed my elbow. I turned.

"Paul?"

"Hey, I've been trying to catch you all night. You've been breaking it down out here." He smiled and his eyes crinkled in that eager-to-please way he had. My hands went cold, and my heart started popping like a popcorn popper.

"Listen, do you wanna step outside so that we can hear a little better?" he asked.

I paused, unsure of myself, but then looked at Margo, motioning toward Paul. She nodded, shooing me on, never breaking rhythm. Adjusting my dress once more, I followed him outside.

The air in the Elks' Lodge parking lot was cool compared to inside. We could still hear the dull thump of speakers. The sweat on my shoulders made me shiver.

"Here," Paul offered. "Do you want my jacket?"

I took it. Paul's jacket smelled of coffee and a strong men's cologne that he must've borrowed from his dad. As I draped it over my damp shoulders, I imagined myself as a character in a movie — this was the moment when the guy gives the girl his jacket, the pre-romantic moment. Then, just as quickly, I reminded myself not to be ridiculous.

"Nice night," Paul observed, propping one foot up on a low wall by the walkway. He gestured toward the full orange moon. I looked at the orange glow hovering over the Melva supermarket, and then at Paul. He'd tried to tame his curly hair with some sort of gel. Now it clung in stiff half waves on his head. It looked terrible, but I appreciated the effort. He had on tuxedo pants but was wearing an old R.E.M. T-shirt instead of a tuxedo shirt — probably something from his older brother — and Chucks instead of dress shoes.

I realized that I wanted to touch Paul — an arm, a hand, anything — more than I'd ever wanted to touch anyone else in my life. I wanted to feel the weight of his breath moving up and down in his chest and — *oh, God! Stop it!*

Paul coughed. "Umm —" He cleared his throat and coughed again. "So the day we went for bagels, I was going to tell you something else, along with the dumb little anthropology paper. And then I was going to try to tell you again the other day too, when we got ice cream. But for some reason I didn't do it then either."

He looked at me full-on with his kind brown eyes. Nervously I jerked at my dress and did a nipple check.

"I was going to tell you then that Susannah and I broke up."

"I heard afterward," I said. "I'm really sorry."

Confession: I was not sorry at all.

"No, it's okay. We didn't get along that well anyway. . . . So I was also going to ask if you needed a Livermush escort. But you never let me ask. And then I felt bad about the list, and I told myself it's probably too late anyway. . . ."

I felt that annoying flush creeping up my neck and onto my face. That's what he'd been starting to say? Impossible. "As friends, right? Well, we've known each other a long time, I guess. Sorry for cutting you off that day. I was . . . well, what you said about me being hypercritical, well . . . I think there's some truth to it. And it hurt my feelings a little because it seemed true. . . . Sorry, side note. Friends?"

He kicked the wall his foot had been resting on nervously. A bit of cement dust wafted to the sidewalk.

"Um, well, friends would have been okay too, I guess. But I was going to ask you, umm, like . . . as a date-date. Wow, this is sounding corny. See? You're not the only one who sometimes hangs back . . . who needs a little push."

"To do what?" I asked.

Just then, there were voices at the door. Missy Wheeler

emerged, walking beside, of all people, Chuck Healey. Chuck Healey! And he looked, well, almost cute in his tux tonight, I had to admit. Missy saw us and waved, looking a little embarrassed.

"Hey, y'all," she called. "Just getting some fresh air."

Paul and I watched them walk out of our line of sight. Paul nudged me and winked.

"I told you he was a good guy," Paul said, smiling. "Your pal Missy thinks so."

"Yeah," I replied, grinning. Daisuke/Chuck was A-OK — at least no weirder than the rest of us. "Anyway, you were saying?"

"I dunno. I get nervous about things and back away, I guess. Like with you."

"Like that night? Like when you needed to feed Barker suddenly?" I asked, thinking of the terrifically embarrassing, formerly unmentionable moment of the Almost-Kiss.

He tilted his head, smiling. "Yeah. Like that. Dumb," he said, studying me in a way that made my throat feel like it was closing off and I could get no more air. "And what I'd actually meant to do was . . ."

He trailed off then and looked down, and I could see even in the streetlight that the rims of his ears had turned bright red. He became preoccupied with a small stone on the sidewalk, kicking it back and forth between his toes. *Almost, almost,* I thought — but this time I didn't feel embarrassed. Just patient.

"A date-date doesn't sound corny," I said. "Am I one of your fads?"

He laughed. "No, no . . . and I'm serious about at least seventy percent of those fads anyway. I'm evolving into a more stick-with-it type guy." He smiled at me.

I smiled back at him. At that moment, that Magic Moment, I felt my stegosaurus shoulder blades blend into my back, and my worried, woolly-worm eyebrows relax into gentle commas, and my skinny frog arms and legs almost look pretty there in the moonlight. . . . And my best possible, self-chosen discount dress, well, it was all right — even *ironically* cool.

"I may have evolved myself," I said. "I may be destined to be something other than an anthropologist anyway. . . . Something else . . ."

"Does that happen? Do die-hard anthropologists change their stripes?"

I shrugged. "Maybe I'm just in the process of becoming a better anthropologist. . . . Regardless, I'm becoming a Woman of Action. Let's go dance."

"Not yet. First I want you to read this," Paul said.

He handed me a folded sheet of paper. Here it is, in its entirety:

```
    Anthropological Observations of Janice Wills
                  by Paul Hansen


 1. The Janice Wills creature is of slight, birdlike
    frame and can be found in her natural habitat
    around the environs of Melva, NC.

 2. She can be recognized by the anthropology book in
    her hand — if she has a freshman anthropology
```

textbook from any university, then she is not
Janice (the actual Janice read all the major
introductory texts years ago).

3. Her aesthetic is nerd-chic-hipster, still in the
formative and slightly fumbling years.

4. She tends to be more comfortable keeping to the
fringe of things, watching others and making
observations.

5. She is hypercritical, so while in her presence
please do not discuss Renaissance festivals or
role-playing games, snort while laughing, or do
anything else that she might deem unbecoming. At
the very least, aim for sarcasm/irony. Also, best
not to have eaten cheese puffs immediately before
seeing her.

6. But she is also sincere, forgiving, loyal, and quick
to apologize.

7. Her preferred foods include fruit-on-the-bottom
yogurt, Swiss cheese, Pink Lady apples, and cups of
dry cereal. Oh, and coffee ice cream.

8. She winces slightly, left eye closing more so
than the right, when her feelings have
been hurt.

9. Even though she claims to be an "ugly duckling,"
this observer finds her to be very pretty. The kind

of pretty that's always interesting to look at, not the boring kind.

10. She has an expressive face (see note on wincing above), and thus would make a terrible poker player.

11. Despite her best efforts to downplay her talents, she's actually smart, hilarious, and fun to be around.

12. She will one day be an excellent anthropologist.

13. I like her. In high school parlance, I don't just like her, I "like-like" her.

After I read the entire list, I kept staring at the paper in my hand. I shivered, but I wasn't cold. It was weird to read all these things, to see that Paul had been noticing them the whole time. It felt like he knew me. I looked up at him. I like-liked him too.

He had smiley brown eyes. Something about the way his face was tilted made me a little short of breath. It occurred to me that he finally might kiss me.

ANTHROPOLOGIST'S NOTE:
The field is in disagreement about the origins of kissing — whether it is a learned or instinctive behavior. It might be related to the grooming behavior that we see in other animals (dogs licking, etc.) or to mothers chewing

food up for their children. True, neither of these options sounds very romantic.

ADDITIONAL NOTE:
Kissing also allows for prospective mates to smell each other's pheromones. Supposedly we are more attracted to people whose genetic makeup is dissimilar from our own. Evolutionarily this is supposed to lead to offspring with greater disease resistance.

I suddenly had the desperate need to cough. His face was very near mine, and I couldn't hold it in. I coughed. Our foreheads hit.

"Ouch," he said.

"Sorry!" I said.

Ordinarily I would have been excruciatingly embarrassed by this — so much so that I would have made an excuse and fled. Instead we both stood there, looking with amusement at each other. We were alone at the side of the Elks' Lodge. I could hear the happy shouting of our classmates from inside, the faint bass thump of the music.

"Take two," he said.

Then Paul's face was close to mine again, and he was kissing me. His mouth was slow and soft and kind, and we only bumped noses once (it wasn't even painful), and when our teeth clicked, I stifled a private giggle, and the whole beautifully awkward transaction went on and on and on, and I felt the long-held tension between us release like the hiss of air from a balloon, and I learned the sweet, specific taste of his fruit-punch mouth.

(I would have imagined the kiss scene for my movie heroine in just the same way — perfectly imperfect, gloriously clumsy.)

We pulled back from each other and stared. Then I burst out laughing.

"What?" asked Paul. "What's wrong?"

"Nothing," I said. "I'm just happy."

ANTHROPOLOGIST'S NOTE:

And that, more than the Miss Livermush Pageant, more than the dance, more than any specific birthday or the prom, was the coming-of-age moment I'd been waiting for. And I had no criticisms. I wouldn't have wished it any other way. I didn't want to rewrite a word.

ADDITIONAL NOTE TO MARK ALDENDERFER, PH.D.:

Although this format may be unconventional, I'm hopeful that you and the *Current Anthropology* editorial board might see something here in my observations worthy of publication in your journal. And I'm always open to further research. I'm learning to be a better anthropologist every day.

ACKNOWLEDGMENTS

Big thanks to my agent, Miriam Altshuler, for finding this manuscript a home, and to my editor, Cheryl Klein, for her help shaping my hopeful jumble into a real book. I couldn't have asked for more insightful readers. More generally, a heartfelt thanks to all those who've encouraged my writing endeavors — fiction, poetry, or otherwise — along the way: in particular, thank you, UNC–Chapel Hill Creative Writing Program, especially Michael McFee; thank you, Johns Hopkins Writing Seminars, especially Mary Jo Salter and Dave Smith; thank you, Corporation of Yaddo; thank you, Bread Loaf Writers' Conference. A huge thank-you to the ever-charming David Prude for his excellent photography. I'd also like to acknowledge the Sarah Vowell segment on the *This American Life* episode entitled "What You Lookin' At?" to which Paul refers when discussing the pinkness of goth. (And if you aren't already a listener, I should add that *This American Life* is a great radio show. You should go listen as soon as you finish reading this page.)

Shout out to Shelby High School and the Shelby High School class of 1998. Shout out to Shelby, North Carolina. Love and gratitude to my hometown girls, Leigh Ann and Rebecca, and to my bff since high school days, Mary Lattimore, who is still one of the most incredible people I've ever had the privilege to know. Love and thanks to my remarkable siblings for being the best in the world: to my clever and hilarious brother Alex, for his title brainstorming help and steadfast enthusiasm; to my wonderful brother Lane, for always supporting me and keeping me hip to what the DJs are playing; to my best sister, Adie, for bringing me extra sweetness and light when I need it. Pearson siblings, you rock the party that rocks the party. And of course, most of all, thank you, Mom and Dad, for having been (and continuing to be) my tireless champions since day one. And thank you, Nana and Grandaddy. You're the best. Finally, love and thanks to my brilliant, patient husband, Matthew Smith, for everything, everything, everything.

This book was edited by Cheryl Klein and designed by Phil Falco. The text was set in Centaur MT, with display type set in Modern. This book was printed and bound by R. R. Donnelley in Crawfordsville, Indiana. The production was supervised by Cheryl Weisman. The manufacturing was supervised by Adam Cruz.